ARMOURON™

'Stand Together . . . Battle as One!'

THE ARMOURED GHOST

www.kidsatrandomhouse.co.uk

The Armouron
Don't miss any of the
titles in this awesome series:

The Armoured Ghost

Lying Eyes

The Caged Griffin

Prisoner on Kasteesh

ARMOURON™

THE ARMOURED GHOST

O. B. McGann

BANTAM BOOKS

ARMOURON: THE ARMOURED GHOST
A BANTAM BOOK 978 0 553 82116 1

First published in Great Britain by Bantam Books,
an imprint of Random House Children's Books
A Random House Group Company

Bantam edition published 2010

1 3 5 7 9 10 8 6 4 2

Set in Palatino

Bantam Books are published by Random House Children's Books,
61–63 Uxbridge Road, London W5 5SA

www.kidsatrandomhouse.co.uk
www.rbooks.co.uk

Addresses for companies within The Random House Group Limited
can be found at: www.randomhouse.co.uk/offices.htm

THE RANDOM HOUSE GROUP Limited Reg. No. 954009

A CIP catalogue record for this book is available from the British Library.

Printed in the UK by CPI Bookmarque, Croydon, CR0 4TD

For centuries, an order of knights worked to keep the peace across the galaxy. Mighty warriors, the Armouron Knights fought for Honour, Duty, Compassion and Justice. They battled organized crime and helped defeat cruel dictators. They prevented wars. Life in the galaxy was not perfect, but people knew justice and peace.

Then, on one planet after another, huge corporations began to seize power. They wanted to control the entire galaxy – and only the Armouron Knights were stopping them. The corporations spread lies about the knights, turning people against them. They sent their private armies to defeat them. Terrible battles were fought but, one by one, the Armouron Knights were captured or killed.

Now the last of the Armouron are scattered around the edges of the galaxy. Not many are left, and they are getting old. A new generation is needed. Planet Earth is controlled by the Perfect Corporation. They call it a Perfect World, but in truth, it is a prison. Here, on Earth, one of the last knights has come to find some new recruits and train them as warriors.

Because the galaxy needs the Armouron more than ever . . .

1. Perfect Corporation
2. Gladiator Arena
3. Salt's Workshop
4. Armouron Academy
5. Old School
6. SeeBlock Tower
7. Perfect Vision HQ
8. Nu-Topia Hospital
9. Shopping Mall
10. Peace Keeps
11. Fuel Dumps
12. The Park
13. Waste Dumps
14. Epsilon Power Station
15. Spaceport

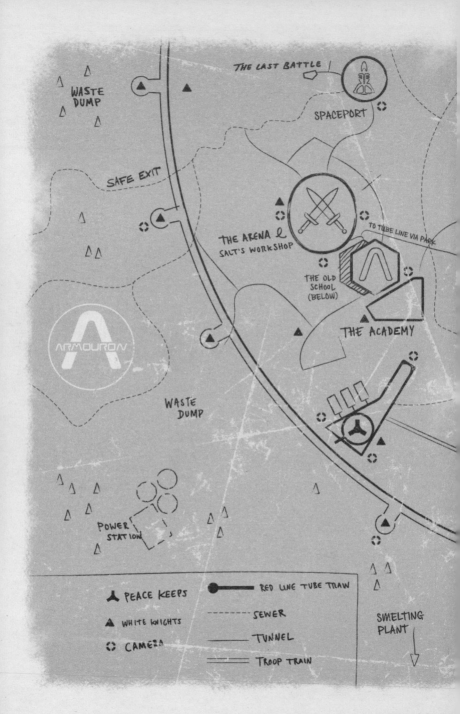

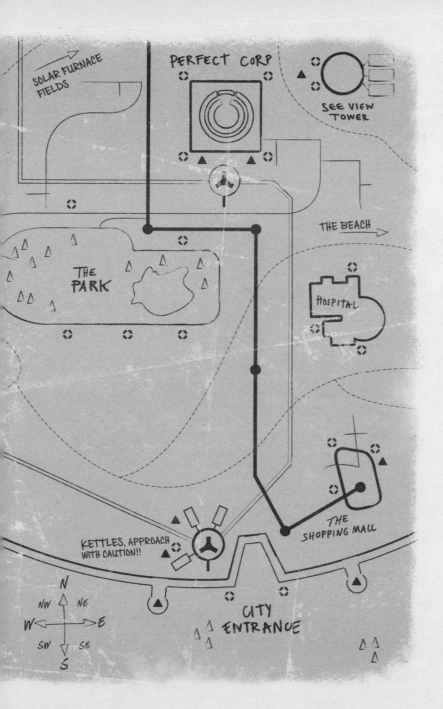

THE ARMOURED GHOST

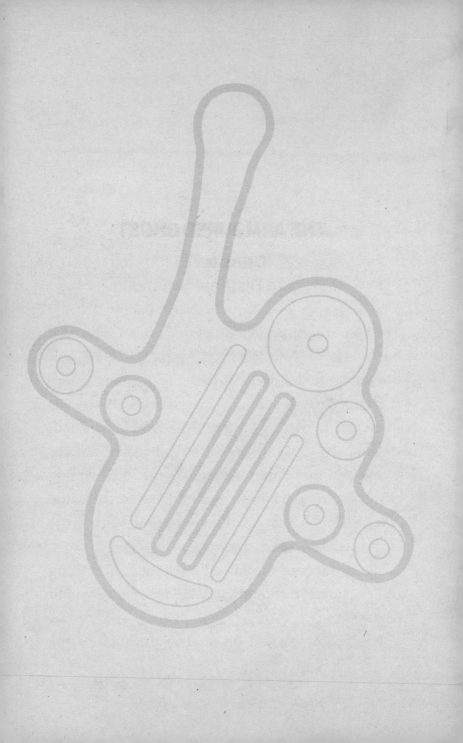

Chapter 1
On a Distant Planet

The old knight knew that this would be his last battle. He was already badly wounded, his red armour battered and cracked. He hobbled down the deserted street, moving as quickly as his injured legs would allow. Whatever happened, the monster must not get the medallions. Ahead of him was a stone temple, dark against the evening sky. It was shaped like a pyramid, but with a wide square top. It was as old and rundown as the empty, ruined town around it.

Heavy footsteps followed the knight. The thing did not hurry. It thought it could take its time. But it was wrong.

The knight backed up against the wall of the

temple, taking wheezing breaths, glaring at his enemy. He had wounds in his shoulder, his side and both his legs. His left arm was broken. But his spirit was still strong. The giant figure stopped in front of him, its shadow falling over him.

'YOU HAVE FOUGHT WELL, OLD FOOL,' the armoured robot said in a cold, mechanical voice. 'STAND ASIDE AND I MIGHT LET YOU CRAWL AWAY AND DIE IN PEACE.'

'I'm not dead . . . not yet,' the knight growled at the machine. 'And I've beaten monsters like you before.'

'YOU'VE NEVER FACED ANYTHING LIKE ME,' the robot told him. 'WHY DO YOU KEEP FIGHTING WHEN YOU KNOW YOU CAN'T WIN?'

'That's the difference between us,' the knight said, gritting his teeth. 'There's more to me than a suit of armour. And it takes more than strength to win a fight. But no walking kettle will ever understand that.'

Wincing with pain, he lifted his sword to swing it at the monster.

'Now, come on! Fight me, you clockwork piece of garbage! Come on!'

The robot attacked, its sword-strikes crashing down on the knight's blade like hammer blows. The old man was shocked by the machine's power and skill. It snarled at him like some kind of animal, grunting as it hit out at him. Robots weren't supposed to do that. He blocked and deflected as many strikes as he could, stabbing at the robot's heavy armour. Then his sword broke and only his own armour saved his arm from being cut off.

Hoping his terror did not show on his face, he held up the stump of his sword, roaring his battle-cry.

'Armouron!'

But it was hopeless. The fight did not last much longer. With a final howl of despair, the knight was smashed against the wall, slumping to a silent heap on the ground. The robot reached down to pull the medallion out of the knight's armour. It gave a low hiss as it realized that the totem was fake. There was no power in this useless piece of metal. It tore the old man's armour apart, searching the body. None of the medallions were there. The knight had tricked him.

The machine heard a sound out beyond the edge

of the town. The distant roar of rocket thrusters. From the forest at the edge of the ruined town, there came a burst of light. A small spaceship was blasting off, rising on a pillar of flame into the evening sky.

The ship disappeared after a few seconds, and then there was a bright flash high above the clouds as it jumped into hyperspace. There was no way of catching it now. The medallions were gone.

The robot looked down at the still form of the knight and let out another hiss. It almost seemed as if the old man was smiling.

'NOT SUCH AN OLD FOOL AFTER ALL,' the machine said.

It had taken the robot over a year to track down the two men who carried the last of the power totems. This dead knight had fought for just long enough to give his friend time to escape with them once more. The robot gave a long, deep growl, but showed no other sign of the anger it felt.

Crouching down, it continued to pull the armour off the knight's body. There were several pieces it could use to replace its own damaged parts. The knight must have given his real medallion to his friend to carry away. That meant that the other knight had escaped with six power totems. One man now had half of the original Twelve. Their loss was a terrible failure, and the robot's master would be furious. But perhaps it did not matter. After all, there was no one left alive to use them.

The time of the Armouron Knights was over.

Chapter 2
Getting Clobbered

Rake watched with giddy excitement as the two armoured Gladiators circled each other out in the Arena. He was supposed to be working – there were floors that needed mopping. But this was too good a chance to miss.

He was able to watch the sparring match through a small window in one of the changing rooms. The window looked out from under a row of seats in the grandstand, where the spectators normally sat to watch the competitions. As a cadet, Rake hardly ever got to watch Gladiators in training. And getting to see Lanista in action, and watch her knock Stamper around, was a dream come true.

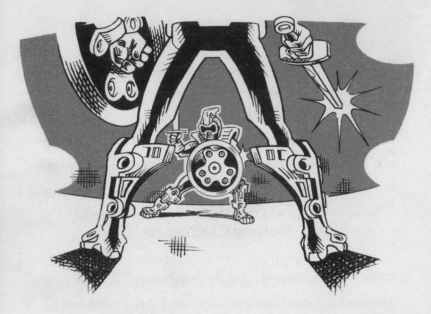

Lanista blocked Stamper's kick and swept his feet out from under him with her sword. The young Gladiator landed hard on his back.

'Yeeesssss!' Rake cheered quietly, shaking the handle of his mop.

'What's going on?' a small voice asked, making him jump.

Standing behind him was a little Far-Eastern girl with white hair. Her name was Snow, and she followed Rake around whenever she had a free moment. He sighed and pulled over a chair for her to stand on so she could see out of the window. Rake had to stand on tiptoe to see out himself.

'Stamper's getting flattened,' he told her as she got up on the chair.

Stamper was back on his feet, moving round the Arena, his sword at the ready. But Rake could see he was on edge now. Lanista had him scared. Every time the warrior woman moved, Stamper flinched like a nervous dog.

'Who's that he's fighting?' Snow asked him.

'How can you *not* know Lanista?' Rake said. 'She's one of the greatest Gladiators this side of the galaxy. People say she was trained by one of the old Armouron Knights, before they all disappeared. Look, this is just training – a practice match. Stamper's always jabbering on about how he's going to slam heads now he's started to compete in the Gladiator Games. This is his first year and I think he's in for a shock.'

Most of the time, Rake didn't mind Snow following him around. A lot of the other cadets were suspicious of her – they thought she was a bit of a jinx. Weird things tended to happen when Snow was around. She seemed OK to him. He was only a Grade Three Cadet, years away from being a Gladiator. But he dreamed of becoming a famous Gladiator and was keen to show off what he knew about their warrior world. This was fine with Snow, because she liked to listen. She was only a Grade Two, and still had a lot to learn about it all. And Rake was good at explaining things, even if he did like the sound of his own voice.

'If *she's* so good, shouldn't you want *him* to win?' Snow prodded her finger into his ribs. 'You know, cheer for the underdog and all that?'

'Nah, I hope he gets clobbered,' Rake sniffed.

'I wanted to show you something,' Snow whispered to him. 'Something I found this morning . . . it's really weird—'

'Hey! That mop's not for leaning on!' a rough voice shouted.

Rake turned to see one of the instructors standing at the door to the changing room.

'Cadet Snow, what are you doing here? I'm pretty sure you have work to do. Cadet Rake, I want to see this floor so clean you could eat your lunch off it – or you *will* be eating your lunch off it. Is that clear?'

'Yes, sir!' Rake barked, slapping his wet mop

down on the tiles of the floor.

Snow jumped down off the chair and, with her head bowed down, walked out past the instructor. The man watched Rake for another minute to make sure he was getting stuck back into his work. Then the instructor touched his finger to the grape-sized phone in his ear to make a call, walking off down the corridor. Rake sniffed. The man was probably calling the office to report the two cadets.

Outside, Rake heard Stamper's body hit the ground again. But the young cadet didn't go to look this time. He just squeezed his mop out into the bucket of dirty water and moved on to the next room.

Rake was tall for his age, with light brown skin and spiked black hair. He couldn't start training as a proper Gladiator for a good while yet. Not until he was fifteen – and then he had to work up to the level of a Grade Five, which was when you got your first suit of armour. But he was already learning everything he could about the life.

There were six changing rooms in this block of the Arena and Rake had to mop out all of the floors. When he was done with the mopping, he had to clean all the toilets in the block before he could break for lunch.

This was how things worked at the Academy. All cadets had to spend at least half their day, every day, working in the Arena. Rake had training after lunch. He lived for training. Even getting to mop the floors in the Arena's Gladiator Block was useful, because sometimes he could sneak a peek at what some of the Gladiators were doing there. Sometimes he could even watch them practise their fighting methods. Cadets weren't allowed to see the Gladiators training. Getting to watch Lanista was worth cleaning a few toilets.

Like most of the other cadets, Rake was an orphan. He didn't know how his parents had died, because he had never been told anything about them. He had been brought to the Academy when he was four years old and had lived there ever since. Once they joined the Academy, cadets were hardly ever allowed out into the city that surrounded the huge complex. At least, not until they became Gladiators – or they failed and were thrown out.

Chapter 3
The Bloodstain

Snow found Rake again when he went to the cadet canteen for lunch. He was late, so most of the others had finished up. Her lunch tray was already empty, but she slid down the bench to be beside him.

'I have to show you this thing,' she said quietly.

'What is it?' he muttered.

He was looking down at the compartments in his tray. There was a grey mush he thought might be potato. Beside that there was an orange mush that was probably carrots. And then there were some brown pellets that were either cat food or freeze-dried meat. Or both. There was also a pale grey cracker that was so dry the cadets sometimes stole them to write secret messages on to each other. He was sure food wasn't supposed to look like this, but cadets were raised on it, so it couldn't be all bad.

'You have to come and see,' Snow insisted.

Rake sighed. He wasn't hungry anyway and he had ten minutes left of his twenty-minute lunch break. Taking a few of the meat pellets to eat on the way, he followed Snow out of the canteen.

Snow did a lot of the same kinds of jobs as Rake. They both worked in Domestic Services, but she was a cleaner in the Arena's hospital most of the time. She led him to one of the wards, a white and green room with eight beds and the soft sound of humming medical equipment. Rake had ended up in rooms like this a few times before, with injuries he'd picked up in training. Some cadets liked going to the hospital – they got to rest from work if they were injured. Rake hated the place. Being stuck in a bed meant he was missing training sessions.

'So . . . what?' he asked.

'This is where they bring a lot of the injured Gladiators,' Snow told him. 'Mad Jack was brought here after his match on Saturday night. You remember how his helmet got knocked off when he was fighting Stamper? And he had all that blood coming out of the cut on his cheek?'

Rake nodded. He remembered it – he watched every match, unless the instructors made him work in the evenings. Stamper had only just started taking part in the Gladiator Games. The fight on Saturday was the first time he had beaten a major star. Mad Jack was a famous Gladiator, but people were already talking about how good Stamper was. They were saying he was the most gifted rookie anyone had seen in years.

'I had to clean the floor afterwards,' Snow told him. 'Normally, the medics clean up the worst of it, so there isn't a lot left to do. They're very careful when it's one of the Gladiators who's hurt. But this time, they left a bandage on the floor. It was the one they used on Mad Jack's cheek. I was walking past and I saw it fall. It went in under that trolley there beside the bed. They didn't spot it when they were clearing up.'

'OK, I know I'm a big fight fan, Snow,' Rake said to her. 'But I'm not the weirdo type who collects used bandages, if you're trying to sell it or anything.'

Snow shook her head. She walked over to a set of cupboards under a counter at the end of the room.

'You know how the instructors search you when you've finished work? In case you've stolen anything?'

Rake nodded. Cadets who worked in the Arena were searched all the time. The instructors never trusted them. Anything that belonged to a famous Gladiator could be sold for a lot of money out in the city.

'I was afraid I'd get searched, so I hid it here,' Snow told him.

She took out a box of bandages and rooted around in the bottom of it. Then she lifted a piece of gauze dressing with a white pad wrapped in it. The pad had a bloodstain on it. Rake smiled. She'd hidden a bandage in a box of bandages. Simple, but clever.

'It's fake,' she said.

'What do you mean?' he asked.

'The blood on the bandage isn't real,' she said, holding it out to him.

'How can you tell?' He frowned, taking the dressing from her.

'The smell,' she told him. 'It smells really sweet, like the fake blood we use in first-aid class. I'd know it anywhere. It reminds me of that really sugary breakfast cereal we get on Fridays.'

Rake held the bandage up to his nose. She was right – it smelled like the fake blood all the cadets had to work with when they were being taught their first aid. He lowered it and stared at it for a minute.

'It's really weird, isn't it?' Snow said. 'Mad Jack's cut must have been fake. But why would they want to make it look like he was hurt in the fight when he wasn't?'

Rake thought he knew why, but he didn't want to say. He wasn't fond of Stamper, but Mad Jack was one of his favourite fighters. Rake hated to think that either of them might have been cheating in the match on Saturday night.

'It's just blood on a bandage, Snow,' he said to her. 'It doesn't mean anything on its own. But, I suppose we could . . . no. Look, just forget it. I'll keep hold of this, just in case. You could get in a lot of trouble if the instructors thought you were nosing around in here. Just forget it, OK?'

Snow looked hurt. She had hoped he'd be more impressed with her discovery.

'OK,' she murmured.

'You were smart to notice it, though,' Rake told her, trying to make her feel better. 'You need to be sharp like that to be a Gladiator.'

'Yeah, sure,' she said. 'Whatever. See you later, Rake.'

They headed off in different directions. They had training next, and Rake didn't want to be late. But as he hurried towards the cadet training block, the discovery of the fake blood was really bothering him. Something dodgy was going on in the Gladiator Games.

Chapter 4
Stick Fighting

The stick was padded, but it still hurt as it smacked into the side of Rake's head.

'Aargh!' he yelped.

'Gotcha!' his opponent cried, cackling to himself.

A light flashed on the end of the boy's weapon to show he had scored a point. Rake raised his own stick into guard position and stopped the next blow before it could hit him in the ribs. He knocked the other boy's stick aside and jabbed him in the stomach. His own stick flashed. The boy grunted and fell to the floor, holding his belly. His name was Hoax, and he was Rake's best friend.

'You OK?' Rake asked.

Even with the sponge padding round the sticks, and the mats on the floor, the cadets picked up plenty of bruises.

'Sure,' Hoax replied. 'This reminds me of that time I was attacked by that tiger in India. It was like these sticks, soft on the outside but hard on the inside. Only with really big claws. I barely escaped with my life.'

Rake rolled his eyes and helped his friend up. Hoax was a hopeless liar. His first reaction to any question or any sign of trouble was to lie. Once you got used to him, you could normally tell when he was actually being honest. Often, it was when he looked awkward and a bit shifty.

With red hair, white freckled skin and pale blue eyes, Hoax could put on an innocent face instantly. But he was loyal to his friends and Rake trusted him . . . most of the time. As sparring partners they were well matched. Hoax was a little younger and smaller, but they were about the same build and skill level. Even so, Rake always had a slight edge.

'How big was that tiger?' Rake asked.

'It was, like, *this* wide,' Hoax exclaimed,

spreading his hands as wide apart as they'd go.

Rake hit him across the chest with the sponge-covered stick, knocking him over again. Lifting his own arms, he held the flashing stick over his head, shaking it in a victory dance. All around them in the training hall, the other cadets paused for a moment to watch Rake parade around his fallen opponent. Snow was there too, over in one corner. Rake had noticed her giving him some funny looks.

'You snea— sneaky clacker!' Hoax coughed, trying to catch his breath.

'That's what you get for lying,' Rake told him.

'Go chew a shoe!' Hoax got to his feet, holding up his hand as Rake came in at him again. 'Hang on a second. Gotta . . . gotta get my breath back.'

They waited there for a minute, as the smacks and thuds of the stick-fighting training went on around them. The instructor looked over, but she didn't shout at them. She knew Rake and Hoax were keen enough – they didn't take breaks unless they really needed them.

'They've moved me to another department,' Hoax said, as he rested on one knee.

'What? Where?' Rake asked.

Like him, Hoax had worked for Domestic Services.

'The Costume Department,' Hoax muttered.

'Where?!' Rake laughed. 'The *Costume Department*? Not even the Armour Department? You're going to be making *costumes*?'

'Keep your voice down, you rump,' Hoax hissed. 'Everybody'll hear!'

Rake smiled, but did as his friend asked. Whenever the Gladiators weren't in their armour, they all wore flashy costumes if they were appearing on television, or in front of an Arena audience.

'At least there's lots of girls there,' Rake chuckled. 'And you'll get to work with some *fabulous* colours and fabrics!'

'Get lost,' Hoax retorted. 'I'll probably meet more Gladiators than you'll ever see mopping floors in the Arena. Mad Jack is in there every other week, looking for his new look. You know they make the costumes for every single Gladiator, right there in that department? Even the ones for warriors that come from other planets. The place is huge!'

Rake was going to point out that this couldn't

✖ ♈ ⬡ ◉ ▦ ⧖ ⬗ ⬙ ◒ ✬

be true. Gladiators came from all over the galaxy. Why would all the costumes be made in one place on Earth? That reminded Rake of Snow's discovery – the fake blood. He hadn't told Hoax yet, but he wanted to. Maybe this evening, when they could go somewhere quieter.

Hoax nodded when he was ready to start again, but as they raised their sticks, Stamper walked into the hall. He was dressed like the cadets in a tunic, loose trousers and a belt with an identity disc in the clasp. But while they wore white, he was dressed in brown, the colour of an assistant instructor.

'Oh, fantastic,' Rake sighed.

Stamper went up to the instructor and said something into her ear. She nodded.

'All right, hold up!' she shouted and the hall came to an immediate standstill. 'I have to leave early. The assistant instructor will finish the session.'

With that, she walked out. Stamper clapped his hands and grinned at them.

'OK, I'm going to show you a new move,' he said. 'I'll be unarmed. Who wants to attack me with a stick?'

A hush settled over the hall. The cadets knew what Stamper was like.

'I'll have a go!' Rake called up.

Some of the other cadets shook their heads. Rake was always first to volunteer – anything to get attention.

'Ah, Rake,' Stamper said, smiling. 'Thought you might.'

Rake quickly moved up opposite the older boy, who held up his hands like a magician to show that they were empty. Rake raised his stick and, in one quick move, swung it down towards Stamper's head. Stamper stepped to the side, deflected the stick with his arm and slammed his forearm back into Rake's chest. As he did, he hooked his foot in behind Rake's ankle, tripping him up. Stamper dropped onto the younger boy as he fell, knocking the wind out of him. He got his victim in a painful armlock. He put it on a lot harder than he needed to.

'I told you to clean my room yesterday, you worm,' Stamper whispered in Rake's ear, so no one else would hear. 'Mess with me and I'll mess you up. Got it?'

Grabbing the hair at the back of Rake's head,

he lifted the younger boy up onto his feet. Rake hissed, trying not to show the pain.

'Right, who wants to see that again?' Stamper asked the cadets.

'I do!' Hoax exclaimed.

Chapter 5
Identity Discs

Rake sat out on the roof of the cadet training block. Cadets were forbidden to come out here, but he needed some quiet time. And from here, he could see some of the city. Nu-Topia. Since joining the Academy, Rake had only been into the city twice – both times, he had been in a group of cadets taken out for a day tour. With their soaring towers and gentle curves, the shining polished buildings of Nu-Topia looked like another world. Sometimes the Academy felt more like a prison.

It had been a hard session that afternoon, finishing up with half an hour on the running machines. Rake rubbed the back of his neck where Stamper had nearly pulled the hair out at the roots. The dinner bell would ring in a few minutes. He'd have to rush his meal if he was going to get out and clean Stamper's room before the older boy got back.

Stamper and some of the other young Gladiators used the junior cadets as their slaves. They got them to do jobs for them, bullied them and sometimes even practised some of their nastier fighting moves on them.

Rake had stood up to Stamper when he first came to the Academy. And ever since, Stamper had targeted him for the worst treatment. Rake lifted his hands to his face. He wasn't a wimp, but Stamper was a Gladiator now. He could make Rake's life a misery. If Rake told on the older boy, nothing would happen and everybody would hate him for being a squealer.

'You shouldn't have offered to hit him with the stick,' Snow said from behind him. 'Maybe if you stop giving him all that attitude, he'll leave you alone.'

Rake looked up. Snow was standing on the concrete slope, behind and to the left of him. Sitting down next to him, she stared at him with her big innocent eyes. Rake often wondered how this quiet little girl had ended up in the Academy, training to be a Gladiator.

'I'll never stop,' he told her. 'Stamper can go and rot. Someday I'll be a Gladiator too, and I'll kick his backside from one side of the Arena to the other.'

'I bet you will,' she said. She even sounded as if she believed it. 'Listen, I was talking to Oddball in training. He was helping me on the chariot simulator. I'm still useless at it. Anyway, you know Oddball works in the Armour Department, right?'

Rake nodded. Oddball was a bit of a geek, but he was OK. He was mad into doing little experiments and liked to make things with bits of scrap he dug out of the bins in the Armour and Weapons Departments. He talked about weird stuff all the time, as if his mind was on some other planet. Rake shook his head. Somehow, it didn't surprise him that Snow and Oddball would be friends.

'Well, I asked him about Mad Jack's helmet,' Snow said. 'You know, to see if they were fixing it. To find out if there was anything strange about the helmet. And he doesn't know about Mad

Jack's armour, but he's been watching the guy who's in charge of making the armour – that old guy, Salt.

'So, Oddball, he's pretty good at making stuff himself. He reckons that Salt is fooling with the armour sometimes. Oddball thinks that Salt is designing some of the armour so that it's *made* to break when someone hits it.' Snow frowned, puzzled by it all.

Rake's face was twisted up, not because he was confused, but because he was getting angrier by the second.

'Why would they do that?' Snow asked. 'Why use fake blood to pretend someone's injured, or make armour that's designed to break when it gets hit?'

'Because somebody's cheating,' Rake growled. 'Gladiators come from all over the galaxy to compete in the Games. When the Armouron Knights disappeared, the Gladiators became the greatest warriors in the galaxy. Billions of spectators watch every fight from the stands or on the web. People can make a lot of money by betting on who will win a fight. Imagine how easy it would be to get that money if you knew someone was going to lose on purpose. Or if they lost because their armour was easy to break.'

He looked out at the city and took a deep breath.

'And the audience loves it when a Gladiator gets hit so hard his armour cracks open. You get extra points for that in a competition. The crowds go wild. Somebody is cheating – they're fixing the competitions so they can make money. And if Salt is messing with the armour, then he's right in the middle of the whole mess.'

Rake stood up and turned towards the door that led into the stairwell.

'There's something else he told me,' Snow said, pointing at the medallion on Rake's belt, the one that marked his cadet grade. 'Our medallions – they're not just plastic discs.'

'I know. They have all our identity info on them,' Rake said.

'And each one has a tracking device,' Snow added. 'If you're wearing your belt, the instructors know exactly where you are.'

Rake stared down at his belt. Any cadet who was found out of their dorm without their belt on was severely punished. He gritted his teeth and headed for the stairs.

'What are you going to do?' Snow asked him.

'I'm going to find out what the clack is going on,' he said.

'Me too,' Snow chirped, as she followed him down the stairs.

Chapter 6
The Investigation

It took Rake a while to convince Snow that she couldn't come with him. It was past lights-out: they were both supposed to be in bed. Cadets caught anywhere outside their dorm rooms after lights-out would catch hell from the instructors. And to make things worse, Rake was leaving his belt under the mattress of his bed. He didn't want to be responsible for getting her in trouble. And he wanted to do this alone.

Creeping along the dimly lit corridors, he made his way to the manufacturing block of the Academy. This was where the armour, weapons and chariots were made for the Gladiators. This part of the complex was made up of workshops and rooms filled with heavy machinery. Some of the lights were still on. As part of their training, the cadets had to learn about each section of the Academy. The large room that Rake had come to was Salt's workshop, and the old man was still working.

The door was only open a crack and Rake peeked through, watching the old engineer. Salt was a tall, stocky man. He looked about sixty, but could have been older. Despite his lined face and grey hair, he looked in excellent shape. There was a welding mask covering his face now. Salt put down the blowtorch he was using to weld a joint in a shield. He took off the mask and sighed, wiping sweat from his face.

A hand came down on Rake's shoulder, nearly making him jump out of his skin. With a thumping heart, he turned, expecting to see one of the instructors behind him. But it was only Oddball.

'Hey! Snow said you'd be here,' Oddball whispered. 'I want to join your investigation.'

He was a big guy, older than Rake, but like Rake he was a Grade Three. Dark-skinned, with short dreadlocks, Oddball wore a pair of goggles that never seemed to come unstuck from his face. Rake wondered if he slept with them on.

' I'm not "investigating" *anything*,' Rake growled back. 'I'm just checking out some stuff. Get lost!'

'Nope,' Oddball said, shaking his head. He always spoke very quickly, as if he couldn't get the words out fast enough for his hyperactive brain. 'You're going to need me. You don't know your way around here well enough. And you don't know anything about armour and materials and chemistry and stuff. If something was wrong, you wouldn't be able to see it. Me, I've got the grey cells.'

Rake was about to argue that he had enough grey cells of his own, when he spotted Salt coming towards the door. He pushed Oddball in front of him into a room on the other side of the corridor, closing the door after them. They watched through a narrow gap, as Salt came out of his workshop and headed off down the corridor, striding along with a walking stick and a heavy limp.

The two boys crept out into the corridor after he was gone, and made their way cautiously into the workshop. The place was filled with workbenches, racks of hand tools, power tools and

pieces of armour. Rake wasn't sure where to start, so he went over to examine the shield Salt had been working on. He recognized it. It belonged to a Gladiator known as The Boulder.

'It's been made so it will break into pieces,' Oddball said from behind him, reaching round to point at it. 'See the lines, here and here? This gets hit and *KA-BAM*! It'll break like a piece of glass.'

'Yeah,' Rake said. 'These are weak seams. The Boulder's going to be in for a real shock when he goes to protect himself with this. So Salt is making *faulty* armour on *purpose*. We have to report him to the instructors. But we'll need proof – something that's small enough to sneak out of here. Let's have a look and see what else we can find.'

They had just started searching around when

Oddball suddenly pushed Rake down behind a workbench that held a huge power drill. Someone was at the door of the workshop. They held their breaths, thinking that Salt had come back. But it was a much smaller figure that slipped in through the doorway. It was a girl, taller than Snow, but shorter than Rake. She moved quickly and quietly around the room, exploring every inch of the place.

The girl was tanned, with an untidy mop of brown hair and a wiry build. Rake and Oddball exchanged looks. They didn't recognize her. She wasn't a cadet. Her clothes were like those of someone from the city. Brown baggy trousers with pockets on the legs, a grey sweater with a hood and grey trainers. The intruder wore no medallion on her belt, no identity disc at all.

She had a backpack with her and she was picking up some of the smaller pieces of armour and tucking them away into her pack. So the girl was a thief. She was coming closer to the workbench, but stopped at one of the computer consoles. Switching it on, she started to use the hologram screen to search the Academy database.

'Grab her!' Rake barked.

Oddball jumped up and went to snatch hold of the girl. She kicked him in the stomach and leaped over the bench – but Rake was already moving around to the other side and he caught hold of her left arm as she landed. She tried to punch him with her right fist. He blocked the strike and spun her round. He forced her against the bench, locking her arm behind her. The girl wriggled and thrashed and spat at him.

'Japes! It's like trying to hold onto a fish!' he grunted. 'You're not going anywhere, I'm good at this. Who are you and how did you get in here?'

'Go smack yourself,' she retorted.

'Are you in with Salt?' Rake pressed her. 'Are you helping him fix the fights?'

'What?' she said, frowning. 'What are you talking about?'

Rake and Oddball looked at each other. If they took her to the Academy's security guards, they'd have to explain why they were in the workshop themselves. Salt would be called for. They'd have to accuse the head of the Armour Department of cheating, right to his face. Suddenly, they were both very frightened. They weren't sure what to do. What if he could explain the faulty armour?

What if the security people were in on it? Then it occurred to Rake that this girl might be useful.

'The old guy, Salt,' Rake said to her, loosening the armlock a little. 'What do you know about him?'

'Not much – but I know he's hardcore,' she replied, giving in a little as she twisted her head round to study Rake's face. 'I . . . I was caught stealing last night, by three of the White Knights.'

The White Knights were the armoured police who enforced the law in Nu-Topia. After the Armouron Knights had disappeared, Earth had collapsed into chaos. Then the White Knights had come along. They were good at their job. There was almost no crime in Nu-Topia.

'It was just a burger from a street stall,' the girl told them. 'I was really hungry, so I grabbed it and ran and they came after me. They caught me in this back alley. I think they were going to bag me up and . . . and . . . make me disappear. It's happened to a bunch of people I know. So, anyway, this old guy was on the street when the White Knights started chasing after me. They caught me in the alley and . . . and I thought I was toast. But suddenly he's behind them, wearing a scarf round his face. Standing there, armed with nothing but this walking stick, telling them to let me go. They went to grab him as well . . .'

Her voice drifted off for a moment.

'And?' Rake asked, loosening the armlock a bit more.

'And he . . . he . . .' She shrugged. 'He clobbered them. It took less than a minute. They had swords and stun-guns and armour and he still beat the dunk out of them. Then he just put his finger to his lips, as if he was telling me to keep quiet about it, and he left.'

'Salt beat *three* White Knights?' Oddball gaped in disbelief.

'Are you trying to wind us up?' Rake snorted. 'Salt? He's gotta be nearly *sixty* years old. He's got a *limp*. You're telling us he broke the law, protected a thief and beat up three armoured policemen? And anyway, the White Knights don't make anyone disappear. If you steal, they put you in prison, that's all. They're the good guys.'

'Yeah, right,' she said simply. 'I'm just telling you what happened. I wanted to know who he was. So I watched him head off and then

🟐 🟡 🔺 🔵 🔘 🔺🔻 🟠 🟢 ⬢

I followed at a distance. I'm good at that – watching without being seen. I trailed him to the parking garage here, saw him get in through a door in the basement and managed to slip in after him without him noticing. I've been hiding here all day.'

Rake let her go. He wasn't sure what to make of all this. She rubbed her arm, looking at them with a sheepish expression.

'I figured I might as well try and steal some Gladiator stuff while I was here – maybe hack into the database. Go for any useful info I could find and then get out. Make a bit of money, you know? Some of this stuff is worth a fortune.'

'What's your name?' Rake asked.

'Tea-Leaf,' she said. 'Or at least, that's what everyone calls me.'

'Right, well, Tea-Leaf—' Rake started to say, but she hopped her bum up onto the workbench, kicked him in the chest with both feet, rolled backwards over the top of the bench and jumped off the other side.

He fell to the floor, gasping for breath. Oddball went after her as she darted out of the door. He was back a moment later, pulling Rake to his feet.

'She's gone!' he hissed. 'And Salt's coming! Come on, let's get out of here!'

But it was too late – they could hear the sound of Salt's limping footsteps coming down the corridor. There seemed to be someone with him. They looked around desperately for a hiding place, and ended up back behind the same workbench.

Salt strode in, leaning on a walking stick. Rake's jaw dropped open as he saw who was with him. It was Snow. The old man was holding her hand, pulling her along behind him. She looked close to tears. Rake clenched his teeth together – she must have tried to come with him after all and had got caught. Salt closed the door behind them. And then they saw him tap a code into the keypad on the wall, locking the door. Their hearts sank. They were trapped.

Chapter 7
Deep Down Underground

The boys watched to see what Salt was going to do with Snow. The old man took his earphone from his ear and put it away in a drawer. Then he went over to a tall rack of tools on the wall. Each tool was held in a set of clips made especially for it. Salt reached for a row of spanners and pulled one out, but it didn't come all the way off the rack. Instead, he twisted it round in a full circle and pushed it back in. The whole rack swung out from the wall, revealing a hidden doorway. Salt went through it, dragging Snow behind him. The rack slid closed behind them, hardly making a sound.

'Now what?' Oddball gasped, looking at Rake.

'We have to help her,' Rake replied. 'We go

in, get her off him, break out of here and tell the Academy bosses what he's up to.'

'Right.' Oddball nodded. 'How are we going to do that?'

'I don't know,' Rake told him. 'I'm making this up as I go along.'

They went up to the rack. Rake had to stand on tiptoe to reach the spanner and pull it out. He twisted it round and pushed it back into place. They stepped back as the rack swung out. Then they went through into the space beyond the hidden doorway. The door closed behind them with a quiet thump and they found themselves in complete darkness.

'Aw, dunk,' Rake muttered.

A small light came on. Oddball was standing there, a tiny torch-beam shining out of the side of his goggles.

'You're not allowed to have that kind of stuff in the Academy,' Rake said. 'Where'd you get it?'

'I made it,' Oddball said.

'What for?'

'For walking around in the dark, stupid,' Oddball replied. 'Come on, let's go.'

They were in a corridor, but one unlike

anywhere in the Academy complex. The walls were made of stone. They were damp and covered in cobwebs. The two boys came to a set of steps that disappeared far down into the darkness. It took some time to walk down, but near the bottom, they came upon a kind of light that Rake had never seen before. Made of metal and glass, it seemed to have a flame inside it.

'What is it?' he wondered aloud.

'It's an oil lamp,' Oddball told him. 'The flame burns on a thing called a wick, which is soaked in oil. The glass keeps air from blowing out the flame, and helps spread the light. I didn't think anybody used these any more. Not in hundreds of years.'

They went on, and came out into a large room at the bottom.

As they stepped out of the stairwell, a massive steel door slammed shut behind them, giving them a terrible fright. Now they were trapped down in this cave-like place.

With their hearts pounding, they gazed around the huge hall they were standing in. It was lit by more of the oil lamps, but was still dark and gloomy. The roof was high and arched, with huge beams supporting it. There was a circle of pillars around the walls and another circle nearer the centre. In the very centre was a round stone table with twelve wooden chairs. A small wooden case sat in the centre of the table.

All around the room were stands holding suits of armour and weapons. Out to one side, there were even what looked like some small vehicles. But this was not Gladiator equipment. Rake had never seen anything like this before. There were other things too, hidden in shadow. Things neither Rake nor Oddball could identify.

'What is this place?' Oddball whispered.

'I don't think this is Gladiator stuff,' Rake replied softly. 'Look at the designs of the armour and the weapons. And the markings on the medallion studs. I reckon this is Armouron gear.'

'I think you're right,' Oddball muttered, gazing around. He went over to examine one of the suits. 'This is atmosphere armour, for fighting in space. Look at the joints! And that's an ice gun. They only work in Arctic climates, where everything's frozen.'

'But how did all this equipment get here?' Rake wondered aloud. 'You know, we're always told the Gladiators rose up to take the place of the Armouron Knights. But sometimes I think the Academy are trying to cover up some of the stories about the Armouron. You can still read about them on the Academy servers – but you really have to know where to look. You see that table, with the pillars round it? That looks like the table the Twelve Nobles sat round – the twelve leaders. But what's it doing here? The last Armouron Knight disappeared over ten years ago. What's any of this stuff doing here? D'you think Salt *stole* it? Maybe he's a thief as well as a cheat. This is . . . is like a whole chunk of history. It should be in a museum or something.'

'This *is* a museum,' a voice told them, making them jump again. 'A secret museum that doesn't take kindly to intruders.'

Salt was standing only a few metres away, still holding Snow's hand. He let her go and she ran over to them. She seemed scared, but was trying hard not to let it show. Salt limped over to them more slowly, stopping before he reached them. He turned to point at the table in the circle of pillars.

'You're right about the table – and about how the true story of the Armouron is being covered up. This hall was once the home of the Armouron Knights,' he told them in a sad voice. 'It was where the Twelve Nobles gathered to meet and plan. But hundreds of knights came here too, from all over the galaxy, for the Council of Peace. This room was once filled with the greatest warriors from a hundred planets.'

He looked over at the three kids. They stared back at him and then turned their eyes up and looked around at their surroundings. They didn't know what to make of this. How could this dark and dusty cave be the home of the Armouron? Both boys had heard the legends – or at least the ones taught at the Academy. The knights of Earth had lived in a mighty fortress whose towers reached up into the skies.

Salt smiled at them, but it wasn't a very happy smile.

'This was a castle once,' he said, as if reading their thoughts. 'The centre of a beautiful city. But that was before it was destroyed by the bombs of the Perfect Corporation. This hall is the core of that fortress, a shelter built deep underground. It is all that remains.

'I've been watching all three of you for a while.

Don't look so surprised – I knew you were becoming suspicious about your lives in the Academy. I was sure you would search for answers, and that your search would bring you to me.'

'Why have you been watching us?' Snow demanded. 'What's going on here?'

'I'll answer all your questions . . . in time. I'm glad you chose not to wear your belts when you set out on your investigations,' Salt told her. 'Even the Academy instructors don't know about this place. And you haven't seen the half of it. Let me tell you a story. It's the best way to explain things. And turn off your torch please, Oddball. Disconnect the battery. We do not use any kind of electrical technology down here. It's too dangerous.'

'What's going on here?' Rake demanded. 'What are you doing down here with all this stuff? Who . . . *what* are you?'

'What am I?' Salt chuckled. 'A fair question, I suppose. But it would be better to ask what I was. You see, years ago, when I put on my armour, I was Claymore, one of the Twelve Nobles. I was an Armouron Knight.'

Chapter 8
A Planet of Prisoners

Salt led them out of the main hall along a wide corridor. The further they got from the hall, the more they could see that there was a maze of tunnels down here. And most of it was in ruins.

They came to another round chamber, smaller than the great hall, but still very large. In the centre of the floor, a shaft several metres wide disappeared down into the darkness. Looking up, they could see that it had once led up towards the surface too, but was now sealed off with a ceiling of solid rock.

It was obvious there had been a massive fight here at some time in the past. There were scars in the rock walls, gashes left by atomic blades, burn marks, even blast craters.

'This is where I was when the last battle began,' Salt told them. 'There were less than fifty of us left – and only three Nobles. This was where we made our last stand.'

He faced the three children, but his eyes were looking at something much further away, deep in the past.

'More than ten years ago, the Armouron still kept the peace across the galaxy. We were warriors who acted as diplomats between the planets. We kept the peace, prevented wars. We organized police forces and fought against corrupt or cruel governments. We lived by a simple code: Honour, Duty, Compassion and Justice. But it was becoming difficult to recruit the next generation of knights. Some of the big corporations wanted to take complete control of the worlds they did business on. There was a lot of money to be made if they could rule the planets and make the laws. The Armouron stood in their way.

'One of the biggest was the Perfect Corporation. You all know who the Chairman is, right?'

'Of course,' Snow said. 'He's the boss of Perfect Corp – one of the most powerful men in the galaxy. He runs the Gladiator Games. The Chairman is an absolute genius. He's the youngest man ever to run a multi-planet corporation.'

'And his sister is the famous Gladiator, Lanista,' Rake added.

Rake was studying the old battleground. There were statues all around the rim of the shaft. He recognized them – or at least the few that were still standing. They were sculptures of the First Twelve – the original Armouron Knights. But most of the statues were pitted with blast damage, missing limbs and even heads. Two of the statues had nothing left but their legs, standing on their low plinths.

'The Chairman is everything you say and more,' Salt agreed. 'He led the multi-planet corps against the Armouron. He turned the people against the knights by spreading lies about them. The corporations had private armies. They hunted down and killed almost all of the Armouron. Some of the worst fighting happened here on Earth. Only a few knights are left now, scattered around the planets on the edge of the galaxy.'

'That can't be right,' Oddball objected. He pointed at the scarred walls of the chamber. 'Even if the Armouron were destroyed like you say, everyone knew the knights kept the galaxy together. Without them; everything would have fallen apart. And I mean, look at this place – the whole planet would look like this if there had been a huge war. And if Earth was all some big dictatorship now, the Chairman would have to have soldiers all over planet to make everyone obey him.'

'You're right.' Salt nodded. 'But he and his sister are both cruel, calculating and power-hungry. They knew that if people suspected the Perfect Corporation had destroyed the Armouron Knights, there would be chaos. But a lot of the planet is still a battle-scarred wasteland – it's just that people aren't allowed to see it. Most of the people living in Nu-Topia were brought here from other planets. They never saw the fighting – they hardly even heard about it.'

He walked around, running his hands over the walls, pointing out the worst of the damage.

'We made our last stand in this chamber. This used to be where the castle's power source was housed. The Chairman's android troops drilled in under us, shut down the power and came up through the shaft here. There were hundreds of them; they were heavily armed and completely fearless machines. We fought them tooth and nail all the way down the corridor, but they eventually forced us into the Council Chamber. We were not easy to beat and we pushed them back. We thought we were winning.

'Then the Chairman's Flying Fortresses launched their final assault. The androids had only been meant as a distraction. The missiles and bombs completely destroyed our fortress and nearly killed us all along with it.

'Only a tiny group of us survived. We got out by disguising ourselves as damaged androids and stealing one of their earth-drillers. We collapsed the tunnel behind us as we went, to cover up our escape.'

The three kids listened, trying to imagine the fear, the chaos of the battle and the desperate escape deep underground, not knowing if there was anywhere safe to surface. It was the kind of story that belonged in the mists of legend. It was strange to hear it first-hand from this sour old man.

'Perfect Corp just lied on all the news reports,' Salt went on. 'It said the Armouron Knights were heroes who died away fighting old enemies. And then the Chairman created the Gladiators to pretend that the galaxy still had warriors who fought for their people – and he made the White Knights to keep control. It was a clever plan, and now most people believe the Gladiators and the White Knights took over from the Armouron.'

He gazed sadly at the ruined statues.

'After I came back, I used my skills as a craftsman to get a job in the Academy's Armour Department. I've spent most of my free time over the last six or seven years fixing up this place. But everything I do has to be done silently, secretly.

'You know that Perfect Corp runs the Academy, and sponsors the Gladiator Games. What you don't know is that its control doesn't stop there. The Perfect Corporation *owns this entire planet*. Tell me, have you ever felt as if you were living inside a prison?'

All three of the kids nodded. Most cadets, even those who dreamed of being Gladiators, found

Academy life hard to bear.

'That's because it *is* a prison,' Salt told them. 'Everything about that place above us is tightly controlled. The Gladiator Games are a pantomime – a show put on for the people of Earth. Because Earth itself is a huge laboratory, and Nu-Topia is the centre of it. Here, the Perfect Corporation tests its most dangerous products before they are sold across the galaxy.

'Very few people on Earth are even aware of this. The only information they get is the information that Perfect Corp lets them see. When the tests go wrong, they can ruin lives – even kill people. But Perfect Corp doesn't care.'

'So the Academy is only part of a planet-sized prison?' Oddball frowned. He believed what he was hearing, but he didn't want to. 'And the people of Earth are the prisoners?'

'Everybody lives the way the Chairman tells them to live.' Salt nodded. 'Like you, they are all tagged with tracking devices like criminals. They are constantly monitored by cameras and microphones. Nobody can get on or off the planet without clearance from the White Knights, and the White Knights are run by Perfect Corp. The

Kettles, we call 'em. If you try to break the rules or refuse to do what you're told, or if the corporation just has no more use for you . . . then you disappear and you're never seen again.'

The three cadets looked at one another. It was as if a fog had lifted. Suddenly, so many things made sense. Life in the Academy was a lot easier to understand once you knew what the place really was.

'The Games were created to keep everyone distracted from what's going on around them,' Snow said quietly. 'To make them think they still have warriors who will fight for justice. To help keep them deaf and blind to the fact they're being used as lab rats.'

'So the competitions aren't real?' Rake asked in a small voice. 'That's why . . . why we're never allowed to watch the Gladiators in training.'

'And why they use fake blood to pretend they're wounded,' Snow said.

'And breakable armour to fake battle damage,' Oddball grunted.

'It's all for show,' Salt told them. 'If you eventually become a Gladiator, that's when you learn the truth. And by then, you'll be trained to obey every order the bosses give you – and you'll do it until the day you die. If you obey, you stand a chance of becoming rich and famous. But you will always be under the control of the Chairman. And if you cross him, he can do terrible, terrible things to you.'

Salt turned round, leaning on his walking stick. There was a solemn, searching look on his face.

'Come with me,' he said.

They followed him back along the corridor and out into the Council Chamber, to the round stone table.

'I am one of the few Twelve Nobles still alive,' Salt rumbled. 'As a Master Craftsman, I am responsible for designing and making new armour – a role that also includes crafting new recruits into trained warriors. I came back here, because this is my home planet. Making Gladiator armour is just a front for me – a cover story. Hardly anybody knows who I really am. I want to break this prison wide open and free the people who live in it. I want to bring down the Perfect Corporation. But it will be a long hard fight and I am old. I don't have the strength I once did. I can't do it alone. We need a new generation of knights.

Young warriors we can train in the old ways.

'You are all here because you are brave and hungry for the truth. Do you want to fight for a better world? I can teach you the ways of the knights, but it will take a strong spirit to keep to the code: Honour, Duty, Compassion and Justice. It is not an easy way to live. It could get you killed. But it offers a great and honourable life. So how about it, my young warriors – will you join the Armouron?'

There was a long, long silence while Rake, Snow and Oddball looked at one another. Was this old man everything he said he was, or could he just be a madman on some insane quest? If they joined him, they would be breaking Academy rules. They would even be breaking the laws of the Perfect Corporation. If they were caught, it would be the end of the only life they knew.

But deep down, they each believed that Salt was speaking the truth. And out of all the cadets he had watched over the years, he had chosen *them* to join him in his fight. They wanted to do something about the prison they were living in – to fight for a better world. And to do it while wearing the armour of an Armouron Knight!

There could be no greater honour. One by one, the three young cadets stepped forward. One by one, they said yes. Salt looked at them and saw there was no doubt in their eyes. These were the right ones.

'Then you will be the first,' he said. 'I'd like each of you to choose one of these.'

Opening the case on the table, he showed them five small metal discs that were set into the lining. Each had a coloured design etched into it. Rake reached for the first one in the line, but then paused. He brushed his fingers across it, moved to the second one, and then the third. This one seemed to glow with a faint light of its own. As he touched it, he let out a gasp. He felt a surge of energy flow through his body. He picked it up, looking at it with awe.

Oddball and Snow came forward. They each chose one of the medallions. They obviously felt the strange sensation too, flinching as they took their discs.

'These are power totems,' Salt told them. 'What you're feeling is what we call "the Flow". It means the totem has accepted you. It has called to you, and its energy will only work through you – no one else – until you die, or *you* choose to pass it on to another. It is a powerful force and you must learn to use it. There are many types of totem, but only twelve of these were originally passed down from the First Knights. Each of the Twelve Nobles carried a power totem. Only the finest warriors could be given one. The totems are given power by each knight who passes them on – and they are priceless. A few are still held by knights on the outer-edge planets. Some have been lost. These are yours – you must use them well. They will enhance your senses, your strength, agility and other talents. You will heal faster.

'They will also enable you to train for hours longer before you become tired. You must continue living your normal lives. I'll arrange to have all of you come to work in my department. We will train at night, while the Academy sleeps.

'I'll design a suit of armour for each of you too. Real Armouron suits, not the clacky rubbish I have to make for the Gladiators. The totem will be mounted in your armour and will act through it. Remember, a totem only works for the warrior it chooses. You may have come looking for me, but I have been looking for you for much, much longer. And there are two more of you still to be found, before the group is complete.

'I'm hoping one of them will be Stamper. He's one of the most gifted athletes I've seen in a long time. A natural leader.'

Rake looked at the others, trying to hide his disgust. Salt took a deep breath. Snow smiled at him, sensing his feelings. The old man could not have been certain they would accept his offer – or if the medallions would accept them. They could report him to the Academy. This was a huge risk for him.

'You stand together, you battle as one,' Salt said to them. 'Now, let's get you out of here and back to your dorms. Leave the totems here. Tomorrow, I'll have you all transferred to work in the Armour Department. You'll be moved to quarters near my workshop. We start training tomorrow night. And believe me, you're going to need your sleep.'

Chapter 9
Don't Make a Fuss

Hoax wanted to know where Rake had been for most of the night. They lived in the same dorm, along with six other boys. Hoax had been unable to sleep, waiting for his friend to come back. And Rake wanted to tell him, but Salt had sworn them all to secrecy.

'Fine, be like that,' Hoax told him, looking off in another direction. 'I'll be getting out of here soon anyway. While you were gone, some of us were picked to go to a Gladiator school on Mars where they feed you chocolate that gives you super-strength and you train against aliens that explode when you hit them.'

'Yeah, good luck with that,' Rake snorted.

His brain was full of a screaming rush of emotions. For as long as he could remember, he had dreamed of being a Gladiator. It had hurt him deeply to learn that the Games, the Academy and the Arena were all just a massive lie. But perhaps, part of him had always suspected it. He wanted to share all of this with his friend. But he couldn't, without telling Hoax about Salt too.

Rake, Snow and Oddball were moved to Salt's department, where they would work from now on. They were moved out of their dorms too, transferred to cadet quarters in the Armour Department.

That first night, they sneaked down to the Salt's workshop, and from there to the underground complex – the Old School, as Salt called it. The three young cadets were tense with nervousness. Salt did not help. His face was as hard as stone. Taking them to a large room off the main chamber, he made them line up and stared at them for a long time. He handed each of them a soft belt with a knot on the front that held their medallions. As they felt the Flow wash away the tiredness of the day, he spoke to them in a harsh voice:

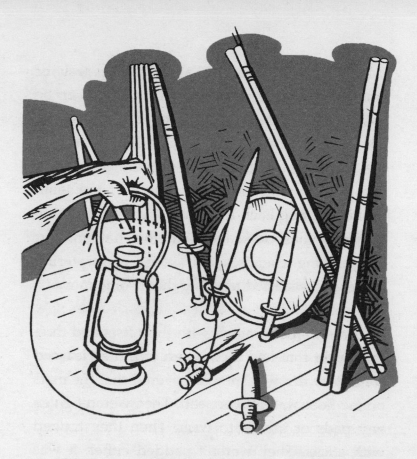

'This will be different from what you are used to in the Academy,' he told them. 'There will be no flashing lights on your weapons, no computer measuring devices. No robotic simulators or holograms. We will train by the light of oil lamps, with simple equipment made from wood and metal and plastic. No electrical power is allowed in the Old School.

'Now, I want to see you jump – knees to your stomach twenty times. Go!'

The cadets did the exercise quickly and easily – it was a standard one in the Academy. But then Salt gave them each a backpack full of weights and had them do the jumps again . . . and again . . . and again. Each time he added a little more weight to their packs. After another half an hour of gruelling exercises and some eye-watering stretches, he started teaching them some moves.

That night, they trained with their fists and their feet. After that had them worn out, they learned some new throws. They discovered that the mats on the floor weren't very soft. They weren't given any pads or gloves to wear. Then they trained with sticks. They weren't padded either. It was becoming clear to them that dealing with pain and exhaustion was a daily part of training to be an Armouron Knight.

And so it went on. By day, they did their normal jobs and their Gladiator training. By night, the three cadets sneaked down to the Old School. Here, they were pushed to their very limits with physical exercises, stretching and endurance training. Salt showed them armed and unarmed moves they had never seen before. They repeated each one until they could do it in their sleep.

Even with the power totems worn on their belts, it was almost more than they could take. When they were too tired to do any more, Salt told them stories, taught them history, geography, astronomy and other subjects they had never learned.

After two weeks, Rake was just starting to get used to the routine, but it was still gruelling. And it was getting harder and harder to keep it all secret. He was already fitter and tougher than he had ever been. He knew so much that he wasn't supposed to know.

Sitting out on the roof one day with Hoax, Rake stared at the city, wishing he could tell his friend all about it. It had been difficult to talk to him recently, because there were so many things he *couldn't* talk about. But today, it turned out, Hoax had something to tell him instead.

'I think you're right,' his friend said. 'You know how you were saying a while back that there's something dodgy about the Games? Well, Mad Jack was in the Costume Department today. He was being kitted out because he's going on a talk show. And you know who came in to see him? The *Chairman himself*. There were some White Knights with him as bodyguards, and they told everyone else to leave. They didn't see me 'cos I was scrubbing out the bottom of one of the wardrobes, so I just kept my head down and stayed there to listen in.'

Hoax leaned in close to Rake, talking in an excited, slightly scared voice.

'The Chairman says to Mad Jack: "You're going to lose the fight on Saturday, Jack. Don't make a fuss about it."'

Hoax looked at Rake, waiting for a reaction.

'Don't you get it?' Hoax said impatiently. 'I'm not lying about this. The boss was telling a Gladiator to *lose a fight*! They're *cheating*! And I don't think Jack was too happy about it. He kept saying that it was "his turn to be champion this year". When he wouldn't stop arguing, the Chairman just gave him this hard look and said: "Lose the fight, Jack, or lose everything. Do you understand?"'

Rake was gritting his teeth. A few weeks ago, he would just have thought that Hoax was lying again. Now, he knew the truth. He was dying to tell Hoax about Salt and the Games and everything else. But he kept quiet. And he was worried – they couldn't do anything to make the instructors suspicious.

'Yeah,' he said at last. 'Sounds weird all right. I wouldn't talk about it too much, though, Hoax. You could get in trouble.'

'Trouble?' Hoax snapped at him. 'We work like slaves and get battered every day so we can become Gladiators. Now I find out the whole competition might be rigged – and you talk about getting into *trouble*? What's wrong with you? I'm going to break out of here tonight. And I'm going to tell the world outside what's going on. People need to know they're being fooled.'

'Come on, Hoax, take it easy,' Rake said, sure that his friend wasn't being serious. 'These guys control everything, there's no fighting them. Let it go, all right?'

'If you're not going to help, you can go and rot,' Hoax snarled. 'I'm leaving tonight after midnight. If you've got the guts to come with me, I'll see you then.'

With that, he stormed off, leaving his best friend

to stare out at the city, doing nothing. Rake knew Hoax too well. His friend lived in a fantasy world – but he wasn't about to try and escape from the only life he'd ever known.

Chapter 10
Oddball's Phone Call

It was Saturday night. Games Night. There were three matches on in the Arena. The main fight was the rematch between Mad Jack and Stamper.

Rake, Snow, Hoax and Oddball headed towards the canteen for dinner. They had just finished training in the chariot simulator. They passed Stamper on the way to the canteen. He was standing in the corridor talking quietly to Salt. The young Gladiator was smiling and picking at his teeth. His earphone rang and he held up a hand to the old man, turning away from him to take the call.

'Please tell me Salt isn't taking him on,' Rake

whispered to Snow. 'I'll chew my own foot off if he joins up.'

'I think Stamper would probably enjoy that,' Snow said.

Stamper was enjoying being a star, and was as cocky as ever. He came in after they sat down with their trays of food. Carrying out his duty as assistant instructor, Stamper walked around the canteen, making sure the cadets ate their greens – whatever the greens were. In a sneaky move, his elbow caught Rake across the back of the head as he went past. Rake winced but did nothing, letting out a quiet growl and trying to act like it didn't hurt. Hoax made a rude sign at Stamper's back.

Snow, who was sitting opposite him, fixed her eyes on Stamper, an intense, hateful look on her face. The others were still staring after the bully, but Rake was watching Snow. Her tray started to shake, even though her hands weren't touching it and the table wasn't moving. The tray began to rattle against the tabletop. She looked down at it, as if noticing for the first time, and it went still. Rake gaped at her, but she just started to eat again, as if nothing had happened. None of the others had seen anything. Rake gave her another glance, but kept quiet.

Oddball smiled at Stamper's back. He drew an earphone from his pocket and slipped it into his ear.

'I've had enough of Mister Big Star,' he whispered. 'I've been dying for an excuse to use this. Watch.'

He spoke a quiet command into the earphone. A little robot on wheels rolled silently out from under the table and scooted after Stamper, happily waving its little arms. As it drew up behind him, Oddball pressed a button on the earphone. The sound of a tacky ring-tone tune beeped out from the little robot. Stamper looked round. The robot exploded, making him jump into the air in fright.

The young Gladiator spun round, losing his balance, and slipped on the remains of the robot. He fell over a bench and onto a table covered in food trays. It all collapsed under him with a crash.

Snow slapped a hand over her mouth to cover her giggles. Most of the other cadets in the canteen had to do the same. Rake actually had to bite his sleeve. Oddball quickly hid the earphone from sight and started munching on one of the tasteless crackers.

'Who did that?!' Stamper roared, as he wiped food from his face and hair. 'I'll find out who did that and they'll be eating floor tiles for the next month of training. You got me? Own up, you rumps! Who was it?'

Nobody else knew who it was and Oddball and his friends weren't about to say anything. Stamper glared around the canteen, but he was out of luck. Rake saw Salt standing near the door on the opposite side of the canteen, watching what was going on. But he didn't step in to help Stamper.

Everybody was talking about the prank as they finished their dinners and left the canteen. Rake,

Snow, Oddball and Hoax were careful not to, until there was nobody else around them and Oddball had dumped his remote control. They still had an hour's training to go in the hologram room. Finally, they were alone in the corridor on the way to the holo-room.

'That was brilliant,' Rake said. 'You're a genius.'

'Thanks,' Oddball replied. 'It was just a bit of fun, really. It's amazing what you can do with just junk – two old instructors' earphones and some spare machine parts. I love blowing stuff up.'

'Pity you had to blow up that cute little robot,' Snow said to him. 'But I'd give a month of dinners to see that look on Stamper's face again. He's going to be a complete demon in training now, though. Rake, don't go volunteering for anything, OK?'

'I don't have training today,' Hoax told them. 'I have some work to finish off. We're making a jacket for the Princess of Jupiter's pet dinosaur.'

'Jupiter doesn't have any princesses or dinosaurs,' Snow pointed out. 'The whole planet's made of gas.'

'Right,' Hoax muttered, as he walked off down a

different corridor. 'Well, maybe I'm just scrubbing the wardrobe floors then. Meet you for the Games when I'm done, yeah?'

The cadets were normally allowed to watch the Games from the windows of one of the empty changing rooms. They got to stay up late too, because the fights were on past lights-out in the Academy. There was the usual Saturday rumble of excitement in the huge complex as the spectators started to arrive. Singers and dancers put on a show while the crowd waited for the competition to begin.

But tonight, Rake was happy to miss the fights. Careful to avoid Hoax and the other cadets, he joined Salt, Oddball and Snow down in the Old School. There, they got on with their Armouron training. It was still a bit strange for them, after life in the Academy. No electric light, no simulators or holograms or robotic opponents. They were forbidden to bring any kind of technology down there – even an earphone or a torch.

The Perfect Corporation monitored the whole planet for illegal power sources. The smallest battery could be detected. Oddball was shocked to discover that even things like his little remote-controlled robot could be picked up.

And Oddball wasn't the only one making robots. Everyone thought the White Knights were humans in armour, but they were actually androids. So were some of the 'humans' wandering around Nu-Topia – androids designed to spy on the people of Earth. They were all connected to satellites that could detect an illegal power source almost anywhere on Earth.

The only electrical power allowed down in the Armouron base was the natural electricity flowing through their bodies. Anything else could give them away. The same would be true when they got their armour and began their missions out in the real world. They couldn't take anything that generated electricity.

Oddball was bitterly disappointed by this. He was keen to start designing gadgets that he could use on their missions. Snow looked happier. She found this new type of training suited her very well. She liked the way everything had to be kept simple. Of all of them, she was improving the fastest.

Above the underground base, in the Arena, tens

of thousands of people were roaring and stamping and cheering for their favourite Gladiators. The stands were nearly full. Stamper was the most exciting new Gladiator people had seen in years. The rematch with Mad Jack was drawing crowds. The warm-up matches were due to start first – less important competitions that got the crowds worked up.

Sitting in a box in the centre of one side of the oval-shaped battleground, the Chairman looked down at it all. A small, slightly round figure, he always dressed well. He was becoming quite vain, but he had a big appetite and little time for exercise. His designer clothes did their best to cover up his pudgy figure. His dark hair was slicked back and his skin was pale. Except for the hard intelligence in his eyes, he did not look like one of the most powerful men in the galaxy.

Hologram displays near his feet showed close-ups of the Gladiators. Sometimes, though, he changed the display to look at the people. They were his people, in the same way that the Arena, the city, the whole planet were his. He owned them all. Then he spoke the words the massive crowd was waiting to hear. His voice was carried over the whole Arena by speakers. It sounded like he was speaking from the sky itself.

'Let the Games begin!'

Down in their deep underground base, the lone Armouron Knight and his three students heard nothing. There was no sound from the huge competition going on above. It was the most important event in the city – and the three cadets no longer cared about any of it.

Chapter 11
Alone in the City

Rake was exhausted when he finished training, but he was concerned about Hoax. Part of him was starting to believe that his friend might be serious about trying to escape. Rake made his way over to his old dorm to talk to Hoax. The other boys were already asleep in bed. Hoax wasn't there. His jacket was gone. Rake could tell by the covers of the bed that his friend had not slept in it. Maybe he had really intended to escape after all. There were only four hours until wake-up call – some of the instructors would be up soon.

Worried now, Rake started searching quietly around his friend's bed. Hoax's belt was hidden under the mattress.

Seconds later, Rake was out of the dorm and sprinting down the corridor.

It took a few minutes to get Oddball and Snow out of their beds and a few more to get down to the Old School. Salt was still there, in the lounge, reading an old book made of real paper. He raised his head as they stumbled to a halt in the doorway. As soon as he saw the looks on their faces, the way they were breathing hard from running, he jumped to his feet.

'What is it?' he asked.

In hurried, blurted sentences, Rake told their teacher about his friend. Salt's face darkened as he listened. He swore under his breath.

'Hoax has made a terrible mistake,' he said. 'If they find out that he's made a run for it, they'll hunt him down. They'll know something's wrong. If he tries to tell people about the Games, he could disappear right along with all the others who've stood up to Chairman. I've been keeping an eye on Hoax. I thought he might be the fourth member of your team. They'll catch him now, and if he's lucky he'll end up in one of the secret underground prisons – if he's unlucky . . . well, he won't even make it that far.'

Salt pushed them back out of the doorway. He began limping towards the workshop that lay off to one side of the training area. They normally weren't allowed in there.

'You aren't ready for the outside world yet,' he told them. 'You're not even *close* to being ready. But we don't have a choice. We have to find Hoax and bring him back before they discover he's missing. But if you run into the White Knights, you won't stand a chance unless you're ready for a fight.'

He turned back to them, waving them towards the workshop.

'I didn't want to do this yet, but if you're going to go out there, you're going to need your armour.'

As they went in, Oddball nudged Rake and pointed. In one corner of the workshop, on a workbench covered in electronics parts, was a box labelled "High Explosives". Rake elbowed him back and shook his head, afraid Oddball might start getting ideas.

In the centre of the workshop, held up on stands, were three suits of armour. One was red and black, the second one was blue and grey, and the third was yellow and black. Their polished surfaces gleamed in the lamplight. Compared to flashy Gladiator armour, these suits truly looked as if they were built for the serious business of close combat.

The three cadets stared at them, their hearts pounding. They could guess from the sizes which suit was meant for each of them. This was it. For the first time, they began to feel like they really could be Armouron Knights.

'These are nothing like the cheap manufactured clack the Gladiators wear,' Salt said, as he pulled Rake up beside the red and black armour and started helping him into it. 'They are crafted from layers of plastallic, a material that bends like plastic but is tougher than steel. This is how real Armouron suits are made. They are lighter, more flexible and tougher than any armour you've seen before. I've made each suit to match your talents. It will take time to learn how each one works – but we don't *have* time.'

Rake was sweating, but he was relieved to find that even though he felt himself trembling through his body, his hands were still not shaking.

'And don't think for a minute that this makes

🕸 🌾 ♨ ● ◉ 🅰 🔸 ◈ ○ ✸

you Armouron Knights!' Salt read their thoughts. 'You haven't earned that title yet. This is a one-off mission. We're being rushed into this and you'll need every advantage you can get tonight. For now, I'll be happy if you don't get yourselves caught or killed.'

Once he had Rake dressed in his armour, he shoved the helmet on the boy's head and snapped the visor down. Then he took Rake's totem and pressed it into place on the armour's breastplate. Rake felt the Flow, the totem's power, surging through his body.

There was a battle hammer and shield to go with the yellow and black armour that Salt had made for Oddball. He picked up the hammer and, without warning, swung it into Rake's chest. The blow knocked the boy off his feet. But as he sat up, Rake was amazed to discover he felt no pain. In fact, the only reason he'd fallen over was that he had been knocked off balance. His chest felt fine.

'Like I said,' Salt grunted. 'This is how real Armouron suits are made. Pick yourself up.'

He handed Rake a sword and shield. With a flick of his wrist, he showed the boy how the handle could extend out to turn the sword into a lance.

'Now, let's get you two suited up,' Salt said to Oddball and Snow. As they rushed to their suits, handling each piece with awe, he added: 'Rake, practise your weapons moves while you're waiting.'

'Come on,' he said to the others. 'Hoax is out there, alone in the city. Every second counts now.'

Chapter 12
Armoured Combat

When the three cadets were all suited up, Salt led them down a corridor they had never seen before. He was still dressed in his Academy uniform. The corridor led to a stairwell, which took them up to another secret door into the Academy. This one opened into the Armour Department's shuttle bay. The department's supply shuttle stood on its launch platform. They climbed on board and took their seats.

It was an ordinary-looking ship, the kind that were used in their thousands, making deliveries all over the planet. It was sleek at the front, but boxy at the back, where the main hatch lowered to form a ramp. Its wings jutted out from the two engines either side of the grey and blue body of the ship, with the tail protruding from the third engine mounted on top. A U-shaped windscreen wrapped around the front and there were two windows at the back, on either side of the hatch.

'The only technology we can use is the stuff that belongs to the Academy,' Salt told them as he strapped them in. 'I fly all over the place in this thing, so we don't need to worry about being spotted. I have ways of disguising it too, if I have to.'

Rake shifted uncomfortably in his seat. The armour was like a second skin, but the seat wasn't made for an armoured passenger. Oddball, in his yellow and black armour, was bigger than Rake and was having a similar problem. Snow looked quite content in her blue and grey suit. Salt sat down in the pilot's seat and started the engines.

'The trick will be to find Hoax and get you in close to him without the White Knights getting suspicious about the shuttle. I can't go with you. If something goes wrong, I'll have to fly in fast and pick you up.' He looked back at them. 'With my leg, I'd only slow you down anyway. Once you're on the ground, you're on your own. Do you understand?'

They all nodded. But the fear was finally beginning to set in. Things were about to get real. Dangerously real.

Salt hit the button on his control stick, setting off the thrusters and blasting the craft out of the bay and into the night sky.

The city lights stretched for kilometres in every direction. Some of the buildings were over a thousand metres high. Some were straight and tall, others were weirder, curving shapes. But they couldn't see most of the buildings – it was just a maze of lights and streets, stretching off to the horizon. Below them, the crowds from the Arena were still spreading out through the streets, on their way home or hoping to make the night last a bit longer.

'It's enormous,' Snow gasped, looking out of the window. 'How are we going to find him down there?'

'I told you before, I've been watching all of you for a while,' Salt replied. 'Hoax has broken out a few times before – but he always came back before they discovered he was missing. There's one place he always goes. I think he'll head for there first.'

Rake said nothing, but was shocked to hear his friend had been leaving the complex without telling him. Hoax must be a better liar than he thought. They flew out over the edge of the sea, where the lights stopped, except for a few scattered boats out on the dark water. Then they swooped back in over a beach and saw the bright coloured lights of a fairground, with roller coasters and other rides, as well as a huge Ferris wheel. The three cadets gaped in amazement.

'I thought you said Nu-Topia was a prison!' Snow cried. 'What kind of dunking prison has a funfair? I've never been to a funfair in my whole life! No wonder Hoax kept breaking out!'

'Don't be fooled by appearances,' Salt told them. 'These rides are all still being tested. Some of them are downright dangerous. Hoax came here, all right. But all he could do was watch. He had no clearance to go inside. Hang on . . .'

He banked hard to the right, using the shuttle's sensors to pick a figure out of the crowd on the ground. The sensors zoomed in on a boy running through the crowd.

'There he is! Look!'

The boy was being chased by four tall white armoured figures. White Knights – Nu-Topia's armoured enforcers.

'They've found him!' Rake shouted. 'We have to help him!'

Salt was already flying back towards the beach. The thrusters kicked up sand as he came in low, stopping to hover over a grassy bank. Here, they were hidden from the funfair by some trees.

'Listen to me,' Salt called to them as the rear hatch lowered down, forming a ramp out of the back of the shuttle. 'If they thought he was from the Academy, there'd be ten times as many Kettles here. He probably just tried to sneak in and got spotted. *But they must not get a good look at him.* Grab him and get out of there. And above all, *do not try to make a stand against the White Knights.* You aren't knights yet – you're not ready. And as soon as they see you, we'll have an army of them down on top of our heads in minutes. Do you understand?'

They all nodded. Seizing their weapons and shields, they got ready to jump.

'If you can't make it back here, I'll pick you up over there!' Salt pointed at a building shaped like

a giant fist, not far from the edge of the funfair. 'In the car park on the far side. Now, go! And remember – Stand Together . . .'

'Battle as One!' they all called back.

Then the three armoured cadets were leaping from the back of the shuttle, landing in the long grass. Rake looked around quickly and started to run towards the Ferris wheel with the others following. The android police were right behind Hoax. He was weaving through the crowd, but the White Knights just charged through, shoving people out of their way.

As they passed under the Ferris wheel, one of

� ♥ ♦ ● ◉ 🅰 ⊘ ⬯ ◉ ✷

them reached out, nearly getting its fingers on Hoax's collar. He twisted aside, kicked out at it and ducked back between its legs. It turned round, snatching at his tunic. But just at that moment, a large hammer smacked into the side of its head, sending it flying. Oddball jumped in between Hoax and the next android, ready to swing his hammer again. The White Knight paused, waiting for its two comrades to catch up. They never did.

It turned to see Rake drop from the Ferris wheel. The cadet crouched, ducking under one robot's sword and deflecting it with his shield. He swiped the legs from under it with his sword. Then he used its head as a springboard, flying over the swinging sword of the fourth White Knight. His knee cracked into the android's cheek, sending it sprawling to the ground.

'Dunk, I'm good!' Rake shouted as he landed, laughing with the thrill of it all.

The one he'd hit in the legs rose up behind him. It raised its sword over his head. Then its own head was cut off by a shield that came slicing through the air. The shield swooped away in a long curve and came spinning back into the hand of Snow, who stood several metres away. The robot's head bounced across the ground, leaving a trail of sparks.

The White Knight that had stopped to wait for back-up was so surprised by the attack on its comrades that Snow and Oddball were able to finish it off easily. Snow swung her baton down alongside Oddball's hammer.

Two of the androids were starting to get up again.

'That's it, we're out of here!' Rake shouted.

'Who the clack are you?' Hoax gasped. He couldn't see their faces through the visors. 'What are Gladiators doing out here? And since when did they let robots join the White Knights?'

'Later!' Rake snapped, looking back at the androids. 'And we're not Gladiators – we're knights . . . sort of. Come on!'

They ran through the fairground, but all around them sirens started up. More White Knights appeared among the rides and stalls. The way back to the beach was blocked. They would have to make for the building Salt had showed them.

'We need to go this way,' Snow said suddenly, pointing off to the side.

'What? Why?' Rake asked.

'I . . . I just think it's the best way to go,' she muttered.

Rake stared at her for a minute. The way she was pointing out wasn't the most direct route. It would take longer. For reasons he didn't understand, he nodded to her.

'Over here!' he called to the others, jumping onto a roller-coaster car as it passed them.

It was just starting to slow down as it hit an upward slope. They all leaped on board and it rolled up to the peak of the track. Rake used the height to take a good look around, noting the

dozens of androids appearing in the park. They were blocking all the exits.

'Where are they all coming from?' he muttered.

Then the breath was taken out of his lungs as the car plunged down the steep slope on the track, tilting round a sharp bend and racing through a loop-the-loop. They whirled out the other side.

'What are we doing?' Oddball shouted over the noise of the wheels on the tracks.

'We're going to jump!' Rake yelled back.

'What?!' the other three shouted back.

'There – where it passes the fence!' Rake roared again. 'Jump! *Now!*'

The roller coaster slowed down . . . a little. Leaping from the car, they flew over the fairground fence and tumbled and crashed into a large clump of bushes on the other side. The sirens were still blaring. This was just as well, for Hoax had no armour and he yelled his lungs out as he landed in a bundle of thorns, swearing at the top of his voice.

As the four cadets dragged themselves out from the bushes, brushing twigs and leaves off their bodies, the sirens got louder and faster. Suddenly, all the fairground lights went off, the rides froze in place and floodlights came on.

'Citizens,' a voice spoke over huge speakers that carried the sound all over the funfair. 'There are criminals in the area. Stay right where you are. Have your identification discs ready. Do not move and you will not be hurt.'

Gun turrets started rising out of the ground at the corners of the funfair. The tramping of armoured feet grew steadily louder, as more and more troops marched into the area. The four cadets looked around desperately, then ducked under the arch of a low footbridge for cover. The noise seemed to be coming from every direction.

'We have to get over to the building Salt told us about,' Rake panted. 'They'll have us surrounded in no time.'

'I think we'll have to scratch that plan,' Oddball said in a cold voice. 'Look!'

Their eyes followed his pointing finger. A huge ship was moving across the sky. It was packed with weapons, shielded with heavy armour. This was one of the famous White Knight airships. A Flying Fortress.

Nearly fifty metres long, it looked like an upturned battleship, with most of its heavy weapons pointing towards the ground. The machine was mostly white, with black and silver detailing. It had wings, but most of its lift came from the six engines that were now pointed straight down so it could fly slowly, searching for its targets.

It passed right over the building that Salt had chosen and hovered there. Dozens more android police dropped from compartments in its belly.

'Well, that sucks,' Rake sighed.

'Japes, they're sending an *army* after us!' Snow groaned. 'Don't you think they're overdoing it a bit?'

'I don't think it's for us,' Rake said to her. 'It's to control all the people in the funfair. They don't know what's going on, so they're trapping the whole crowd. It still leaves us pretty dunked, though.'

'This is why we need technology,' Oddball complained. 'We need to call Salt, tell him there's a change of plan. Anybody see a web console?'

'They listen in on all the phones,' Snow reminded him. Then, in a quieter voice, she added, 'I think it'll be OK. I think help is nearby.'

'You guys know your way round the city, right?'

Hoax asked them. 'I only know one way home from here. I'm already lost. You've got somewhere to go if you don't get picked up, right?'

That was when it dawned on them how much trouble they were really in.

They had no way of getting home.

They were lost.

And they were being hunted by an army of battle androids. They could still hear the tramping sound of feet all around them.

Nobody said anything for a moment.

'Hey!' a voice called out in a hoarse whisper.

They looked around, but didn't see anything.

'Over here!' the voice said again.

Less than twenty metres from them, they saw a head and an arm sticking up from the top of a litter bin. The arm was waving at them. Not knowing what else to do, they went over. It was a girl – the same girl Rake and Oddball had caught in Salt's workshop. Rake had to think for a moment before remembering her name – Tea-Leaf.

'Get in!' she said, disappearing down into the bin.

Rake looked doubtfully at the others, then peered into the bin. The bottom had been cut out of it, and the hole led down into a tunnel below. They didn't need to be told twice. Anything was better than waiting up here to be caught by the android police.

There wasn't time to wonder how Snow had known to head in this direction. They were all just grateful for this piece of luck.

The space that Tea-Leaf led them down into was a sewer pipe that was only just big enough for the armoured cadets. Tea-Leaf fitted a cover back up under the litter bin, sealing the hole. Then she crawled along the pipe, leading them into a wider tunnel where they could stand up. It disappeared into darkness in both directions. The only light came from a lamp that Tea-Leaf was carrying. It was like a small version of the oil lamps Salt used in the Armouron base.

'Hey, Tea-Leaf,' Hoax greeted her. 'Thanks a million. You saved our hides there.'

'No problem.' Tea-Leaf shrugged.

'You two know each other?' Rake exclaimed.

'Sure,' Tea-Leaf said. 'We met before, outside the fairground. I like watching it too, but I've never managed to get inside. I was looking for him when your little war broke out up there.'

Rake, Snow and Oddball opened their visors so that the others could see their faces.

'What the–' Hoax gaped in amazement. 'What are you guys doing here? And why are you wearing *armour*?'

'I can't believe you've been coming out here without telling me!' Rake said, ignoring the question.

'You're having a go at *me* for keeping secrets?' Hoax shouted back. 'You're wearing *armour*! You've got . . . got *weapons*! What's going on with you?'

'You want to start walking while you're arguing?' Tea-Leaf asked, pointing down the tunnel.

'We don't take orders from *you*!' Rake said, his fear giving way to confusion and anger.

'Right,' she retorted, as she turned round and started walking. ''Cos you were doing so well on your own. I'm going. I know this city inside out. I can get you home. You can come with me – or stay here, lost in the dark. It's up to you.'

The cadets followed her, their arguments put on hold until they could get back to safety. The march of heavy feet overhead reminded them that their hunters weren't far away.

'Here, listen – are you going to answer me or what?' Hoax asked his friends in a frustrated voice as they all walked away down the tunnel. 'How come you're all wearing *armour*?'

Chapter 13
An Old Enemy

The Chairman was a young man – the youngest ever to control a multi-planet corporation. And the Perfect Corporation was one of the most powerful in the galaxy. He was still standing in his luxury viewing room high on the side of the Arena. The fights were over, the crowds had left. On the screens around him, he was watching the video recorded by the White Knights in the fairground.

For the first time in years, the Chairman felt a shiver of fear. Every police android could record what it saw. And even though the fight at the funfair had taken only a few seconds before the attackers escaped, there were enough clear shots of the criminals. The Chairman froze each screen at a different point. He squinted at them, trying not to lose his temper. He had a very bad temper.

Each screen now showed a still image of an armoured figure using an old-fashioned weapon. There were three of them – plus a boy whose face had not been picked up clearly by the White Knights' cameras. None of them had identity discs.

'Armouron,' he breathed. Waving a shaky hand at the screens, he tried to look more irritated than nervous. 'How . . . how can they be here? What are they doing here after all this time? When I . . . when I flatten someone into the history books, I expect them to stay there. I'm not having this. I'm not having it at all.'

He gazed out of the window at the dimmed lights of the Arena, the rows and rows of empty seats. He had pretended to be as excited as the crowd when they watched the Gladiators prancing around in their imitation of combat. But seeing the knights in action on the screens brought back bad memories of real battles. The Armouron had almost succeeded in capturing him once. He had seen their skill in battle first-hand – he took this new threat very seriously indeed.

Behind him, a tough-looking man in a suit stood there saying nothing. He knew that his boss talked to himself. The Chairman wasn't expecting anyone to answer him.

'Perhaps, more importantly . . .' his boss wondered aloud. 'More importantly, where did they go? We could ransack the whole city, I suppose. Turn everyone out of their houses. Tear down whole buildings if we had to . . . But that would make it look as if we were *scared* of something. It would look as if *something was wrong* in Nu-Topia. No, that wouldn't do at all. We must keep up appearances after all, mustn't we?'

He went quiet, holding his hand to his forehead in a thoughtful pose. He had practised this pose and could do it perfectly. The way he was nervously chewing his lip spoiled it a bit. The tough-looking man in the suit still said nothing.

'I think we need a quick and tidy, but *devastating* solution,' the Chairman said at last. 'I believe we have just the thing. Yes, indeed. Did you notice that these new Armouron Knights were a trifle short? Hardly more than children, I would say. Yes . . . killing them should be easy, I think. Have the shuttle ready. I need to visit the Freezer.'

'Yes, sir,' the tough-looking man replied.

The man showed no sign of the fear he felt at the mention of the Freezer.

The trip in the Chairman's luxury shuttle took only a matter of minutes, but they came down in a very different part of the city. The spacecraft landed gently on the roof of a massive dark grey block of a building with sloping walls. Its only windows were slits around the top. The enormous elevator came right up under the shuttle and lowered it into the building. Then a piece of the shuttle's floor dropped down and into the building. Carrying the Chairman and his bodyguard, the section of floor shot down a shaft at high speed. To the two men, there was no feeling of movement at all.

The shaft took them deep underground to the Freezer. It was here that the Perfect Corporation kept its experimental weapons. And the Chairman's most dangerous inventions. The moving section of floor stopped falling and moved sideways instead. It carried them down a long, long corridor. Heavy security barriers opened in front of them and closed behind them.

Some of the things that were down here could never be let out.

Others chose to stay locked down here.

They came to a steel door that was nearly a metre thick. The Chairman held his eye to a scanner and spoke into a mike. The door swung open. It was freezing cold inside. There, in the centre of a large circular room, was a barrel-shaped chamber. With a hum and a clunking sound, it split apart and opened up as the Chairman approached. Gas hissed, flowing out across the floor like a fog. Lights flickered on.

Inside was an armoured robot, hooked up to cables and tubes. But this thing was nothing like the White Knights. Compared to this machine, the android police were clockwork toys.

This was the Armournaut.

It was alive and it was terribly powerful, cruel and clever. Its life-force had come from a knight who had betrayed the Armouron – a fearsome warrior who had died hundreds of years ago. That knight's spirit had been captured in a medallion. It was this totem that gave the machine life. This Thirteenth Medallion was at least as powerful as the ones passed down from the First

Twelve Knights. Maybe more powerful. Even the Armournaut's body was built from the armour of dead knights. The Chairman gave a little gulp. This machine had been created centuries ago. He had no control over this armoured ghost.

'I am sorry to wake you,' he said. 'But we have a problem. The kind of problem you enjoy solving.'

With a wave of his hand, a screen appeared in the chamber. The images of the young Armouron Knights came up on the screen. The Armournaut gazed at them for a few moments.

'I WILL DESTROY THEM FOR YOU,' it said. 'ON ONE CONDITION: I KEEP THEIR ARMOUR . . . AND THEIR POWER TOTEMS.'

The Chairman rolled his eyes.

'No,' he said. 'You can have the armour. But if those medallions are three of the Twelve, then they're mine. We've been over this before. They are valuable to me. You don't *need* any more power totems. You can only use the one that's inside you anyway.'

'YOU WOKE ME UP TO SOLVE YOUR PROBLEM,' the monster said. There was a nasty edge to its voice now. 'I KEEP THEIR ARMOUR AND THEIR POWER TOTEMS.'

The tough-looking man who stood behind the Chairman bit his lip. He was not feeling very tough at the moment. His hand went inside his jacket, ready to draw his gun. It was a silly thing to do. Guns were no use against the Armournaut. The only kind of gun that bothered this robot needed a tank to carry it. The Armournaut turned its eyes towards the bodyguard. The hand came out of the jacket.

'All right,' the Chairman sighed. The machine's hunger for the other medallions was a problem he would have to deal with at another time. 'You can keep the totems. Now, how will you find them? It must be done quietly – and they have managed to escape our detection.'

'THAT IS BECAUSE YOU HAVE BECOME LAZY AND ARROGANT,' the machine told him, turning its eyes back to him. 'I NEED ONLY TO MAKE THE RIGHT PEOPLE SCREAM, AND THE ARMOURON KNIGHTS WILL COME RUNNING INTO MY ARMS.'

The Armournaut stood up and pulled itself free of the connecting cables. Without another word, it strode out of the room.

Chapter 14
The Last Two

Salt stood before the five kids with his head hanging down on his chest. They were lined up in front of him in the main chamber of the Old School. Rake, Snow and Oddball had taken off their armour. Hoax was looking around in wonder. Tea-Leaf was restless and suspicious.

She had led them through a maze of sewers, tunnels and basements to the Academy garage. From there, the five had made their way down into the Armouron base. Salt had been waiting for them, relief written on his face. Now he was looking very serious indeed.

'I sent you three out before you were ready,' Salt grunted to his cadets. 'If Tea-Leaf hadn't come along when she did, you and Hoax would have been caught or even killed. Things turned out all right in the end, but it was just plain luck. And we can't count on luck.'

He stepped in front of Hoax and Tea-Leaf.

'You two know who and what we are now. We need two more and I believe you're the ones we're looking for. Will you join us?'

'What's in it for me?' Tea-Leaf asked.

'You will receive training as an Armouron Knight and live life by a code that will see you through hard times,' Salt told her. 'You become part of a group of true friends. Apart from that, there will be years of hiding away, being hunted. You will face a high risk of being injured or killed. And a slim chance that, at the end of it, the people of Earth might thank you for saving them from a cruel tyrant. But I wouldn't count on that bit. So, how about it?'

'Wow, talk about making an easy life for yourself, huh?' Tea-Leaf quipped.

'I should tell you, young lady, that I do not have a sense of humour,' Salt informed her. 'I consider it an overrated quality.'

'No, really,' she said. 'Sounds good. I'm in.'

'Yeah, I'm cool with that,' Hoax responded.

Salt gave a little smile. They weren't being as casual as they thought: he knew they would stand by their words.

Rake frowned. Tea-Leaf had never done any Gladiator training. How could she start from scratch now, as a knight? Still, it could have been worse.

'So, Stamper's not in?' he asked.

'No. He's not made of the right stuff,' Salt replied bluntly. 'Now, it's time for our two new cadets to choose their medallions.'

He brought over the wooden box, which held the last two power totems. Tea-Leaf and Hoax both hesitated – if they took turns, only one of them was going to get to choose. The two of them chose at the same time, each picking a disc in one smooth move. They both flinched as the Flow rushed through them – a mixture of energy, emotion and the faint whisper of someone else's memories.

'Stand Together,' Hoax murmured.

'Battle as One,' Tea-Leaf added in a soft voice.

'They have accepted you,' Salt told them. 'We have our five. From now on, you will live by the

Armouron code: Honour, Duty, Compassion and Justice. But none of you are knights. Not yet. And before I let any of you out of here again wearing an Armouron suit, you're going to need a lot more preparation.

'Tea-Leaf, you are welcome to stay down here for the rest of the night. The rest of you need to get back to your beds. Hoax, I'll have you moved into quarters in the Armour Department as soon as possible. So, all of you – sleep tonight, if you can. From tomorrow night, we're going to get serious about your training.'

As they walked back towards the stairs leading to the Academy, Rake said beneath his breath:

'What, like we weren't being serious before? What's he going to do us now?'

Chapter 15
A Bunch of Misfits

Once more, the row of cadets stood before Salt. He walked up and down the line. He did not look impressed. Tea-Leaf and Hoax were trying to hide how nervous they were. They had spent the rest of the last night and day wondering what the old knight had in store for them.

'This is what I've got to work with,' he growled. 'A fine bunch of misfits, I must say. Look at you: a show-off, a thief, a geek, a liar and . . . and a little girl.' Snow looked a bit hurt. Salt looked like he didn't care. 'Well, we're all stuck with each other now, so we have to make do with what we've got. Not one of you is putting on a suit of armour again until I think you've well and truly earned the right to wear it. Let's see if we can whip you into some kind of respectable shape before the White Knights find us and bury us in the darkest prison in the deepest hole on Earth.

'Cadets! Up against the wall! Give me handstand press-ups! And I want to see the tops of your heads touch the floor and then I want those arms perfectly straight! Twenty times! Now!'

The five kids tipped up into handstand positions against a bare piece of wall and started lowering their heads to the floor and back up again. And so began a new level of training for all of them. Gruelling physical exercises to strengthen their bodies. Drills and sparring to improve their speed and coordination. Meditation to help them focus when they were completely exhausted.

For two weeks, Salt used every minute he could spend with them to work them until they dropped. Then he taught them how to pick themselves up so he could work them some more.

By the third week, he decided they were ready to start training in their armour. For the first time, Tea-Leaf and Hoax got to see what the old knight had made for them.

Like the others before them, they each looked

at the tough polished surfaces of their armour. And, for the first time, saw the knights they might become. All five cadets brushed their fingers over the plastallic plating. They could feel the power of the totems flowing through the skin of their armour. They hefted the weapons in their hands, admiring their weight and balance. Finally, Salt had decided they each had earned the right to wear the armour of an Armouron Knight.

All of the cadets were suited up and given the weapons they would use in combat. They struggled to contain their nervousness, their excitement, as Salt walked down the line. He described the qualities of their armour to each of them.

Rake stood proudly in his red and black armour.

'You carry the most weapons in the group,' Salt told him. 'Your suit is designed for strategy and offence. It has a range of small hand-to-hand and throwing weapons. The suit's gauntlets can fold down into wrecking-ball-style fists to deliver devastating punches. Your armour has a selection of maps of Earth on microfilm slides that can be viewed with the helmet's visor. The visor itself comes with a selection of magnification lenses for studying the environment – close-up and at a distance.

'Your main weapon is your short sword, whose handle extends out so that it forms a lance.'

Tea-Leaf was admiring how light and flexible her grey and black armour was.

'You are the spy and scout,' Salt declared. 'Your armour's light-sensitive material can change colour, reflecting its surroundings, which offers a very effective camouflage. Equipment includes lock-picks, a manual microfilm camera loaded in the helmet, and climbing gear. The suit also carries a digital storage device for carrying software for hacking and downloading viruses. But once it's plugged into a computer, there is a serious risk of detection. Built for silence and speed, your suit is the lightest and most vulnerable suit of armour.

'Your main weapon is your crossbow, which has a dagger in the handle.'

Oddball was examining all the features of his yellow and black armour.

'You are the scavenger and engineer,' Salt informed him. 'Your suit is the heaviest in the group. It is built to make best use of its environment. The suit carries a wide range of tools and a small selection of basic chemical compounds. It also has sockets for channelling power and electrical signals. These connections will allow you to hook into most forms of technology, but always at the risk of being detected. The vents in the helmet will enhance your sense of smell many times over, making you an effective tracker and allowing you to identify a wide range of materials and chemicals. As with Rake's helmet, your visor comes with a selection of lenses.

'Your main weapon is your warhammer, which breaks up into different tools.'

Hoax was already fiddling with his orange and black armour, wondering what kinds of tricks it had up its sleeves . . . and any other places.

'Your roles are deception and misdirection,' Salt growled, pulling the boy's helmet up and making him stand straight. 'Your armour plates are sprung to give them a counter-punch quality. If someone hits them, some of the force of the blow rebounds back at them. You can also jettison armour plates in order to slip out of an attacker's grip. The suit's helmet can amplify your voice – so you can make good use of that overactive imagination of yours. Secret compartments in the armour will enable you to trick your opponents. You can spread oil or ball bearings on the ground to cause your opponents to slip, or toss a smoke bomb and disappear.

'Your main weapon is a stick that breaks into a nunchaku.'

Hoax pulled the stick apart, revealing that the two halves were joined by a chain. He practised swinging it around his body.

'Finally you, Snow, are responsible for protection and evasion,' Salt said to the smallest in the group. 'Your armour is almost as light as Tea-Leaf's armour, but is much tougher. It offers the best defence of all the suits. It can protect you against extreme heat and cold. It is light, to allow you to move easily. The low friction surfaces will make it hard to keep hold of you. A fold-away hang-glider can be fitted onto the suit's back, and there are roller-blades in the soles of your boots. You also carry basic medical supplies and your shield can be expanded to three times its size, allowing you to shield others.

'Your main weapon is your baton, which can also fire a climbing rope.'

Snow looked at the T-shaped baton, careful not to release the safety catch on the weapon's trigger.

Salt stood back and stared at them long enough to make them uncomfortable.

'The suits will improve your strength and speed and your senses. They will make the most of your talents. The visors will help you see through illusions and spot magic when it is being used against you. You need another few days to get used to training in your armour and to practise with their features,' he said. 'Then we go outside. I don't need to tell you, that's when things really get tough.'

Chapter 16
A Desperate Message

The day had finally come. Salt had received a cry for help and decided his young students were ready for their first mission. Carrying their armour in packs, they walked up the tunnel to the secret entrance into the Armour Department shuttle bay and sneaked on board Salt's ship. Once the hatch was shut and they were all belted up, Salt hit the thrusters and all six of them were shoved back into their seats as the craft roared out into the night sky.

They flew out over the maze of lights marking buildings and streets. Up there, they circled among all the other ordinary shuttles travelling across the vast city. Salt engaged the autopilot and they put on their armour. The cadets were still getting used to this – some of the pieces were tricky. This time, Salt put on his too – a green and black suit that was scarred by countless battles. His totem was already attached to his chestplate, but he took it off for some reason and fiddled with it. He held it up to his ear, then pressed something on the back, before fitting it back into its socket.

'This might well be a wild-goose chase,' he said to them, as he sat back down in his pilot's seat. 'But we have to check it out. For the last few days, I've been picking up a message on a radio channel that hasn't been used on Earth for years. It's the Armouron emergency channel. The message is badly broken up, as if it was sent using damaged equipment. Have a look.'

He brought it up on the shuttle's main screen. The image was fizzing and distorted, but they could see the face of a figure in a suit of armour. His visor was up and there was fear and determination on his face. They could tell from his armour that this was an Armouron Knight.

'I'm not dead . . . not yet,' the knight growled at the screen. It flickered, disappeared in a rush of electronic snow, then came back again. 'There's more to me than a suit of armour.' The image and sound crackled into nothingness, but came back again. 'And it takes more than strength to win a fight. But no walking kettle will ever understand that.'

The image disappeared, but they heard a terrible despairing wail before the static took over. Salt switched it off.

'It's been playing over and over again,' he told them. 'There's no telling when it was recorded.'

'That guy . . .' Rake said quietly. 'I think I know him, but I can't remember where from. His name is Karn. He's really familiar somehow.'

'You've never met him,' Snow said, reaching out to touch the medallion on Rake's chestplate. 'But I think . . . I think you're wearing his power totem.'

'She's right,' Salt said, giving Snow a curious look. 'Karn was the last knight to wear it. That totem has a lifetime of his memories soaked into it and you're picking up on some of them. This man was one of my oldest friends. Karn gave his medallion to me before I came here. We had six totems and we were being hunted across the galaxy by a creature – a living robot – of terrible power. The Armournaut. An armoured ghost, centuries old, devoted to wiping out the Armouron Knights.

'I was badly wounded and the Armournaut had almost caught up with us. The future of the Armouron was in our hands – we had to stop that monster from getting the totems. So Karn stood and fought the thing while I escaped with the totems. I was certain that he was dead. The Armournaut disappeared not long after the Armouron did. I heard that it had been destroyed in a huge space battle on the edge of the galaxy.'

Salt looked down at his hands.

'I'm still not sure Karn's alive, but I have to find out. I've traced the signal to discover where it's coming from. It's right on the outskirts of the city. It could be ten years old, or he could have sent it a few days ago. There's no way of telling.' He raised his head. 'It could also be a trap. But if Karn is alive, we have to help him.'

'Then let's do it,' Rake said.

Salt flew as close as he dared to the area he had picked out. Then he landed in a deserted street, gliding the shuttle in under a bridge where it would attract less attention. They had to run the rest of the way, nearly two kilometres through dark streets, alleys and tunnels. Salt did his best to keep up, but his damaged leg slowed him down. The cadets stayed with him, but they were impatient to get to the source of the signal and solve the mystery.

Tea-Leaf ran ahead, checking the way was safe. It was her job to find new ways round if the route was blocked or if there was a chance they might be seen, or spotted on camera. But she knew that people did not normally stay out late in Nu-Topia. The White Knights did not allow it.

There were a few of the android police out, but the Armouron warriors steered well clear of them. Eventually, they came to the building Salt had been looking for. It was a factory, an enormous, long building in the shape of a woodlouse. Its roof was built of massive, curving arcs that overlapped each other. There were small windows up on the sides of the arcs, but no other easy way of seeing inside.

'Tea-Leaf, Snow, check out the roof – try and get a look inside,' Salt commanded. 'Oddball, find a door we can open without too much noise. Hoax and Rake, keep watch. If anything happens, we meet back here. If we get split up, we meet back at the shuttle.'

They were all heading in different directions when Salt called them back.

'Wait,' he said. 'There's something you might need to do.'

He pointed to a public web console just outside the gate of the factory. The old knight gave them a phone number. He made them all memorize it.

'If . . . if things go bad on us, I want you to call this number. I'll give you a signal when you need to do it. I'll say the words "I'm not dead yet." Got it?'

'Whose number is it?' Rake asked. 'Why aren't they here now? How . . . how are they going to get here in time if we have to *phone* them?'

'Just do as I say, boy!' Salt growled. 'Now, you've got a job to do. Get on with it.'

Oddball quickly found a lock he could open and quietly slid back the heavy metal door. Salt went in first, with Rake following close behind. Oddball stayed just inside the door, waving Hoax in. Salt and Rake moved further inside. They drew their swords and took their shields from their backs.

It was dark. The only light came from the windows above them, looking out on the night sky, but their visors made it much easier to see. The pair looked up and spotted Tea-Leaf and Snow coming in through a skylight high above them, ready to drop down on ropes. Salt gave his orders with hand signals. They were to stay put for now.

He told Hoax and Oddball to stay near the wall. Rake followed his master on into the factory. It was a massive space filled with rows and rows of different kinds of machines. Conveyor belts, power tools and robotic arms.

They heard a scream – a terrible wail. Moving faster through the machinery, they saw a figure huddled against the far wall. It was a man in a suit of armour. It was Karn.

'No!' Salt muttered.

'I'm not dead . . . not yet,' Karn growled. 'There's more to me than a suit of armour. And it takes more than strength to win a fight. But no walking kettle will ever understand that.'

'He's said that before,' Rake whispered.

'Look closer, lad,' Salt grunted. 'Your visor is

not fooled by holograms. This is a recording. We've walked into a trap!'

Suddenly, eight White Knights rose up from hiding places around them. They fired stun-guns at Salt and his cadet, but the weapons had no effect on their armour. The White Knights quickly drew their swords.

'They should have come packing bigger guns,' Salt said. Then he bellowed: 'Let's take these Kettles apart!'

The androids rushed them all at once, but there were so many of them, they got in each other's

way. Salt cut two of them down in that first clash, his sword moving so fast it was just a blur. Rake stood with his back to his master, blocking, swinging and stabbing, as the Kettles' blades seemed to come in from all directions.

But then Hoax and Oddball were attacking the White Knights from behind. Oddball smashed bodies and limbs with his hammer. Hoax swept his stick right and left to clear a path, then he split it into a nunchaku. Spinning it on its chain, he cracked heads and broke joints. From high above, a crossbow bolt shot down and hit one of the androids in the head. The White Knight collapsed. Snow and Tea-Leaf dropped down on ropes, landing on the remaining android. Snow struck with her baton and shield, Tea-Leaf with the dagger pulled from her crossbow. In seconds, the fight was over.

The warriors stood panting for breath, weapons still raised. All around them, the White Knights lay in pieces.

'Don't think much of their ambush,' Rake snorted. 'They didn't know who they were messing with.'

'No,' Salt said, looking at the hologram of

Karn, still flickering near the wall. 'This was too easy. They knew exactly who they were messing with. And they're not done yet. That was just the warm-up.'

A monstrous figure dropped down behind him, making hardly any noise. It struck Salt on the back of the head, sending him sprawling to the floor.

'THAT'S RIGHT, OLD MAN,' the Armournaut said. 'TIME FOR THE MAIN EVENT.'

It was taller than any man – taller than a White Knight. Its grey armour jutted with ribs and spikes. Its head was long and seemed to be decorated with tubing and horns. Its narrow, curving, slanted eyes glowed a toxic green. It had a shield mounted on its left arm and held a sword in its right hand.

'I thought you were dead,' Salt groaned, trying to get to his feet. His head was spinning. 'I heard you were floating in pieces out in dead space.'

'THAT WAS THE STORY I WANTED PEOPLE TO TELL,' the Armournaut told him. 'I HAVE FEW ENEMIES LEFT. BUT IT SUITS ME TO HAVE THEM THINKING I'M DEAD. THAT WAY, THEY DON'T SEE ME COMING.'

'Well, we see you now,' Rake snarled. 'Stand Together!'

'Battle as One!' his team-mates yelled together.

'Rake, no!' Salt shouted.

The young warrior leaped into the air, his sword coming down in a perfect arc towards the robot's head. The thing did not even raise its sword. It met the blow with its shield, drove the edge of the shield into Rake's stomach and then smacked him across the head with it, knocking him onto a conveyor belt. The boy lay there, groaning.

Oddball came at it next, his hammer humming through the air. Again, the Armournaut just used its shield, deflecting the strike. Oddball quickly reversed the move, swinging his weapon back to strike again. Before he could finish the swing, the monster kicked him in the chest. He was hurled across the floor, crashing into the wall.

Tea-Leaf fired her crossbow – once, twice, three times. The robot let the first two bolts just bounce off its armour. It jammed its sword into the ground and caught the third bolt, flinging it back at Tea-Leaf. The force of the throw was hard enough for the bolt to pierce her armour. She only just got her shield up in time and found herself staring at the point as it punched through and stuck there. When she dropped her shield again, the robot was standing right in front of her. It knocked her out with a single punch.

Snow jumped in to hit it over the back of the head with her baton. She swung the edge of her shield into the back of its neck. The Armournaut didn't even look round. It reached down as she landed, grabbed her foot and swung her like a rag doll, tossing her across the room. She bounced off a conveyor belt and crumpled to the floor.

Hoax was trembling as he came forwards. He'd had time to see all of his friends beaten. The Armournaut was growing impatient. It pulled its sword out of the ground and strode forwards. From a slot in his left gauntlet, Hoax fired some ball bearings at the thing's feet. The robot slipped and stumbled. Hoax leaped at it, swinging his nunchaku. His weight was enough to knock it off balance, but even as the monster fell, it seized the spinning stick and whacked it off Hoax's head. The boy staggered back and the Armournaut kicked him into a piece of machinery.

It was just getting off one knee when Salt attacked. The robot managed to block three lightning-fast strikes, but the fourth caught it a glancing blow across the head. Then Salt kicked its shield aside and drove his sword into its chest. The Armournaut let out a hiss and fell back onto one knee.

'You let the young ones live,' Salt sniffed, gripping his sword to try and pull it out of the robot's chest. 'That's not like you.'

'I HAVE USES FOR THEM,' the thing replied. 'AS A TEAM, THEY HAVE POTENTIAL. BUT YOU ARE TOO OLD TO BE OF USE.'

Salt heaved at his sword again, but it would not come out of the robot's chestplate.

'YOU HAVE DELIVERED YOUR BEST BLOW,' the Armournaut rumbled. 'AND I AM STILL ALIVE. AND NOW I HAVE YOUR SWORD.'

It hit him with its shield, the edge of it buckling the armour over Salt's stomach. Grabbing its sword, it stood up and rained mighty blows down on the old warrior. Each strike of its sword cut deeper into his armour and shield. It was all Salt could do to stop the blade from cutting him in half. One by one, the five cadets began to recover their senses. They rose to find their master on his knees, his shield raised above him.

With one sweep of its blade, the Armournaut cut a chunk off the shield and knocked the helmet from Salt's head. The robot reached down to him, taking a grip of the old knight's chestplate and ripping it off. Salt screamed as his armour came apart. The Armournaut still had Salt's sword stuck in its own chestplate. It pulled the plate off and tossed it away. It replaced it with Salt's, fitting the piece of armour into the sockets in its chest. Salt's power totem gleamed in the setting on the chestplate. The old knight stared hard at it.

'GIVE IN TO YOUR DEATH,' the monster said.

'Hah! I'm not dead yet,' Salt gasped through gritted teeth.

Hearing those words, Rake looked over at Oddball and Tea-Leaf, who were nearest the door. They nodded and hurried out. The other cadets crept closer, ready to help their master, but he waved them back.

'YOUR TIME IS PAST, OLD MAN,' the monster said. 'YOU GROW WEAKER WITH AGE, AS I GROW STRONGER.'

'Maybe,' Salt muttered, looking once more at his power totem. 'But you're not getting any smarter. And now you're plugged in.'

The Armournaut raised its sword one last time. The blade came down with awesome power. Rake barely got his sword there in time, blocking the robot's strike. The impact nearly knocked his weapon from his hands. He grabbed the Armournaut's wrist to stop the robot swinging its sword back at him. The machine raised its left arm to slam its shield into Rake's head, but Hoax got the chain of his nunchaku round the robot's arm, stopping the blow. The two boys couldn't hold its arms for long, but then Snow was there. She threw all her weight against the backs of its knees. The Armournaut toppled over backwards.

It let out a roar, smashing the young knights out of its way as it rose to its feet.

'PERHAPS I'LL TAKE OVER THE TRAINING OF YOUR YOUNG KNIGHTS!' the Armournaut bellowed at Salt. 'THEY HAVE SPIRIT! BUT THEY'RE WASTING THEIR TIME WITH A RELIC LIKE YOU. THE ARMOURON ARE DEAD. I AM THE FUTURE!'

The robot picked up its sword and shield. It seemed as if nothing could stop the machine.

Outside, Tea-Leaf got to the web console first,

switching it on. She started tapping the number in, but then hesitated, struggling to remember. Oddball staggered up behind her and punched in the last few digits.

A tacky ring-tone suddenly beeped from the Armournaut's new chestplate. It froze, looking down. The medallion was ringing like a phone. Salt waved at the others to get down.

'That'll be your future calling,' he told the machine.

Then he covered his head with his hands.

The Armournaut felt an instant of shock before it exploded. Rake and Hoax dived across to their

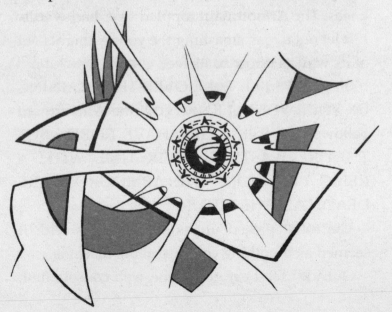

master as the robot continued to erupt into flames. They dragged him away, protecting him with their bodies. The flames caught hold all over the factory, the fire spreading quickly. The remains of the Armournaut's metal skeleton clanked around, crashed into some machinery and then collapsed.

Snow dropped in front of the three huddled figures, expanding her shield to cover them all as another explosion ripped through the factory.

Outside, Tea-Leaf and Oddball gaped at the factory, as fire burst from the high windows and they heard the sounds of more detonations inside.

'Japes!' Tea-Leaf gasped. 'Was that supposed to happen?'

Oddball just stared, speechless. They both broke into a run, rushing towards the building, hoping there was still enough of their friends left to save.

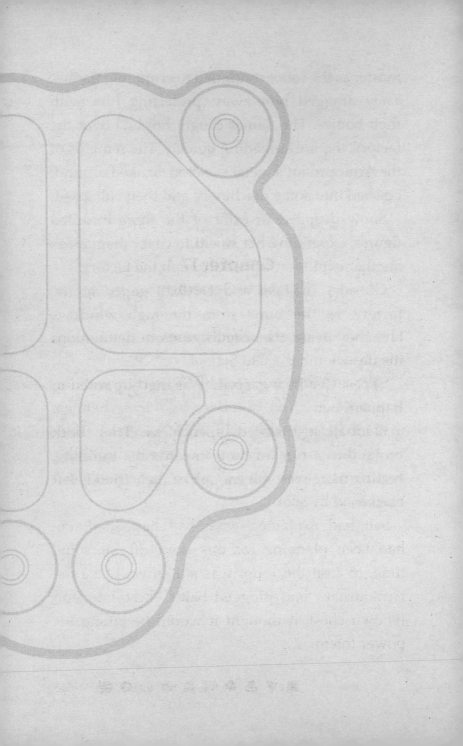

Chapter 17
The New Generation

Hours later, six exhausted figures trudged down the tunnel into the Old School.

Salt was badly hurt, but he insisted on walking without help. The cadets carried their helmets in their hands, along with their weapons. They worked their jaws to clear their throbbing eardrums. Their faces were scorched and blackened by soot.

Salt had explained what had happened. He had been planning for this stand-off for some time, in case the robot was still alive. Once the Armournaut had plugged Salt's chestplate into its own chest, it thought it would be taking his power totem.

Instead, the robot had plugged itself into a remote-controlled bomb.

Salt had replaced his totem with a detonator made using an earphone. He had rigged his chestplate with explosives. He'd got the idea from seeing Oddball's remote-control robot explode behind Stamper.

But he couldn't use a battery in the earphone without being detected. So to set off the bomb, Salt's detonator needed electricity from the robot's body . . . and somebody had to call the phone.

Salt lined the five cadets up in front of him. They stood before him, their heads hanging on their chests. They were bruised and battered and they could barely stand.

'Hold your heads up,' he said to them. 'Be proud of what you did tonight. You fought one of the most dangerous creatures in the galaxy and you won. You all showed bravery, intelligence and skill. It was an honour to fight with you. But I am getting too old for this malarkey. It is time for a new generation of Armouron. I wasn't fighting with cadets in this battle. You fought like the knights you are. It is time I gave you the titles I've chosen for you. You will use them whenever you go out into the world as Armouron Knights.'

He stepped up in front of Rake, placing his hand on the boy's shoulder.

'Templer, the Fearless.'

Snow was next. He put his hand on her shoulder.

'Alida, the Shieldmaiden.'

Next in line was Hoax. Salt rested his hand on the boy's shoulder.

'False-Light, the Trickster.'

After Hoax was Oddball. The master squeezed his shoulder.

'Sappar, the Inventive.'

And finally, Tea-Leaf, the only one who had not grown up in the Academy. Who had never been part of anything before. She avoided Salt's eyes as he took her shoulder. He tipped her chin up with his other hand.

'Balista, the Shadow,' he said. Then he turned to face all of them.

'Lift your heads high and be proud, young knights. You are the future of the Armouron.'

He turned and limped towards the medical bay, wincing at his injuries.

'And you'd better make a good job of it,' he growled back at them. 'Or I'll make you wish the Armournaut had won that fight.'

Chapter 18
The Beating Heart

The Chairman walked slowly through the burned wreckage of the factory. He didn't care about the ashes that soiled his expensive shoes, or the way the pieces of wire and metal snagged on his trousers. It was early in the morning. The fires had been put out, but the ground was still warm beneath his feet.

The White Knights were controlling the area around the factory. The Chairman's staff waited nearby for instructions. He ignored all of them. It didn't take him long to find the first remains of the Armournaut. Some of its metal skeleton had survived the heat of the fires, the impact of the explosions. But the Chairman was not interested in the skeleton. Using a warped steel bar, he poked around in the ashes. If his enemies really were Armouron Knights, they would know the Armournaut's history. But there was a chance that the fire had been too fierce for them to take the robot's heart.

After nearly half an hour, he found what he was looking for. It was an egg-shaped piece of metal, about the size of the robot's fist. It had tendrils hanging off it, making it look like a large spider. There were crystal sections in the shell and light could be seen glowing through them. Peering through a clear section of the shell, the Chairman could see the Thirteenth Medallion inside, giving off a throbbing glow.

This was what made the Armournaut so hard to kill completely. You could destroy its armour, even its body, but nobody had ever managed to destroy this. The Chairman held it up and his eyes narrowed. He allowed himself a slight smile.

The heart of the armoured ghost was still beating.

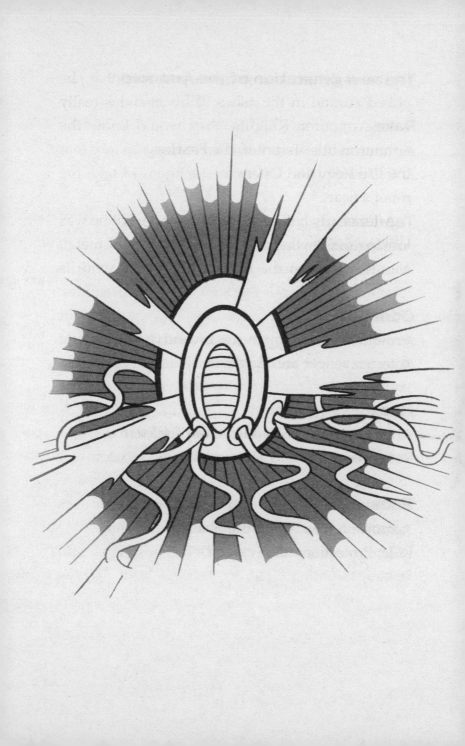

The new generation of the Armouron

Rake
Armouron title: Templer, the Fearless
Role: Strategy and Offence

Tea-Leaf
Armouron title: Balista, the Shadow
Role: Spy and Scout

Oddball
Armouron title: Sappar, the Inventive
Role: Scavenger and Engineer

Hoax
Armouron title: False-Light, the Trickster
Role: Deception and Misdirection

Snow
Armouron title: Alida, the Shieldmaiden
Role: Protection and Evasion

The Armouron master
Salt

Armouron title: Claymore

Role: Master Craftsman and Teacher

The Armouron Code:

Honour, Duty, Compassion and Justice

If you enjoyed *The Armoured Ghost*,
you might like a sneak preview of the
next book in the series: *Lying Eyes*.
Turn over for the first chapter . . .

LYING EYES

O. B. McGann

A BANTAM BOOK 978 0 553 82196 3
Copyright © RDF Media Ltd/Armouron Ltd, 2010

Chapter 1
Across a Dark City

Keep moving, no matter what, don't stop. Rake repeated the words, over and over again, in his head as he ran. This was a race he didn't intend to lose. He was part of one team, along with Snow and Hoax. They were heading for their home, the Old School, through the dark streets of Nu-Topia.

Tea-Leaf and Oddball made up the other team. It was the middle of the night and they were all on a training exercise. Their master, Salt, had left them out in the centre of the city. Wearing their armour, they had to make their way through several kilometres of streets as fast as they could, avoiding the White Knight security patrols and the street cameras. And they had to avoid being spotted by any civilians who might also be out.

They were all still getting used to this strange, dangerous life. The gruelling training, the hiding away, the armour and weapons – these were all parts of their secret new identities as Armouron Knights. And their master had given them knights' titles to go with those identities – Templer, Alida, Sappar and False-Light. But by day, Rake, Snow, Oddball and Hoax lived a very different life.

These four lived penned up in the school known as the Academy. There, they trained to perform mock fights for the crowds who watched the Gladiator Games. It was more theatre than battle. As Armouron Knights, they had to fight for real. Nobody in the Academy knew about their secret second life, except for their master, Salt.

The four Academy cadets had been out in Nu-Topia alone before – but they had never gone this distance across the city. It was scary and exciting at the same time. The competition was all the more fierce because Rake had a point to prove.

Tea-Leaf, the fifth member of the group, had

not grown up in the Academy. The orphan, who had been given the Armouron title of Balista, had lived on the streets, raised as a survivor, rather than a fighter. As far as Rake was concerned, she had yet to earn their trust – and prove herself as a warrior.

Rake was leading his two friends along a narrow alley. He came to a corner and peered out at the street it led into. There was a camera on the top of a pole halfway down the street. He pointed two fingers towards his eyes and then pointed at the camera.

'We have to find another way round,' he whispered.

Snow and Hoax nodded. They were glad to have a rest – Rake had been running them hard. He put a hand up to his helmet and clicked a switch down. A map of this part of the city slid down in front of his eyes. His red and black helmet carried old-fashioned microfilm maps that could be viewed through his visor. The young knights couldn't use computers, phones or GPS on their missions. The Perfect Corporation, led by a creepy genius known as the Chairman, tried to control all the technology on Earth. It controlled all the electrical power in Nu-Topia, The smallest battery or power source could be detected by its satellites.

Rake found the street they were on and quickly picked out another route. This was the part that worried him. He and his fellow Academy cadets were all strangers to the city. They had to use maps to find their way around. But Tea-Leaf had grown up here; she knew the streets and the short cuts. She had an edge over them, but Rake was determined to stay ahead of her.

Oddball would slow her down a bit. He wore the heaviest armour – carried the most equipment. But he wasn't slow enough to reassure Rake.

'Back down this way,' he said softly to the others, 'and then right. We have to cut back across Tar Street and head through the park.'

Without waiting for their replies, he set off running again. Snow and Hoax looked at each other.

'"We have to cut back across Tar Street and head through the park,"' Hoax muttered in a perfect impression of Rake's determined voice. He flicked up his visor to look at Snow. 'Huh! You'd almost be tempted just to let him run off on his own, wouldn't you?'

'Yeah, except he's the one with the *maps*,' Snow replied, raising her visor to gaze back into Hoax's face.

'Good point,' he grunted. He turned and broke into a run. 'Suppose we better catch up. You know what he's like when he gets all competitive.'

Snow moved alongside Hoax, falling quiet as she kept pace with him. Her blue and grey armour was one of the lightest in the team, but like the others, she also carried a weapon in her sheath and a shield on her back. She was the youngest of the group, and didn't have the same stamina as the two older boys running with her. She was having a hard time keeping up.

'Tea-Leaf's going to win anyway,' Hoax said, 'unless we *cheat* somehow.'

'We're supposed to be Armouron Knights,' Snow reminded him. 'You know – we fight with honour?'

'Ah, I'm sure even the old Armouron pulled a few sneaky moves in their time,' he grunted.

Snapping their visors down, they caught up

with Rake, who was looking back impatiently. Leaping over walls, keeping to the shadows, darting from one piece of cover to another, they made their way towards the park that Rake had found on the map. Along the way, they had to wait twice to let White Knights go past. The tall white robot police had to be avoided at all costs. They also kept a watchful eye out for Flying Fortresses, the White Knights' air patrols. The three were all breathing hard when they reached a building site that lay by the road on one side of the park.

Creeping through the half-finished building, Hoax was first to get a view of the park. He immediately ducked back inside. With his left hand, he pulled his shield off the back of his orange and black armour. His right hand hung ready over the handles of the nunchaku in his sheath. The other two moved up beside him. They looked out through a square gap in the wall, where a window would soon be fitted. The three young knights gazed past the bars of the scaffolding outside, stunned by what they saw beyond.

Towering over the park was a giant machine. It squatted on four massive jet engines and was

covered with gun turrets. It must have been over forty metres high. Its engines alone were over half that height. They were jutting out on all four sides like legs, with the main part of the machine looming up from the centre like an armoured building.